Find more of my work at my blog:

www.theauthorstack.com

Find all my work at my website:

www.russellnohelty.com

Bookbub:

https://www.bookbub.com/profile/russell-nohelty

HOW TO CULTIVATE A THRIVING AUTHOR ECOSYSTEM

Embrace your natural tendencies to build a flourishing author career

By:
Russell Nohelty

Edited by:
Lily Luchesi

Proofread by:
Toni Cox

INTRODUCTION

This book is based on **The Author Ecosystems Archetyping System** methodology created by Monica Leonelle and Russell Nohelty in 2023.

I've written a lot of books, but this one didn't come out of a passion project or a sudden bolt of creative lightning. It came out of confusion, frustration, and a weirdly persistent problem that refused to go away.

Monica Leonelle and I spent years working with authors by that point. Between us, we'd helped thousands of writers launch books, build audiences, grow mailing lists, run campaigns, and scale creative businesses. We'd co-hosted masterminds, launched group coaching programs, and walked authors through the entire path from zero audience to six-figure success.

We thought we knew what we were doing.

In fact, we were pretty dang confident in our system, especially after the success of our first flagship program, *The Kickstarter Accelerator*. We helped more than 125 campaigns raise over $1.2 million in our first year. Some authors doubled their income. Others quadrupled it. There were people who launched books that would've sat on their hard drives forever if not for the structure we helped them create.

And yet, for every big win, we saw something strange: a baffling number of authors didn't make it to launch at all. Some had amazing books. Others had big platforms. But even with all the tools, templates, checklists, and coaching—we were only seeing about 20% of our students meet or exceed expectations. About 20% underperformed. And a staggering 50%? They never even hit publish.

That made no sense to us.

We built what we thought was a bulletproof process. The authors who implemented it succeeded. The system worked. So why were so many people still stuck?

We couldn't figure it out.

We looked at the data. We compared case studies. We tracked what platforms people were using. Some authors crushed it on Kickstarter but flailed on Amazon. Others had tiny email lists but absolutely dominated their launches. Meanwhile, there were writers with huge followings and beautiful books who couldn't move a single unit.

It was maddening. We kept circling the same questions:

- *Why are some people doing everything "right" and still failing?*
- *Why are others breaking the rules and succeeding anyway?*

Eventually, we had to face the truth: the answer wasn't in the *tactics*. It was in the *people*.

The breakthrough came when we stopped thinking of marketing as a set of tasks and started looking at it as a pattern of behaviors. We realized that the most successful authors weren't following a single, universal path. They were leaning into their own natural marketing instincts.

Monica and I were the perfect example. She thrived on consistency, systems, and audience-building over time. I lived for momentum, launch cycles, and creative sprints. When we stopped trying to force each other into a single marketing style, our collaboration got way smoother—and way more profitable.

So we started mapping out the tendencies we saw across our students, our peers, and ourselves.

We saw clear, repeatable patterns.

Some people were driven by trends and high-volume output. Others were methodical builders. Some needed the intensity of a launch deadline to stay focused. Some built slow-burning communities. Others thought in systems and brands and immersive worlds.

Eventually, we mapped these tendencies onto the five major ecosystems found on Earth:

Desert. Grassland. Tundra. Forest. Aquatic.

It wasn't just metaphorical. It worked.

Every ecosystem had strengths, weaknesses, natural pacing, and ideal platforms. Suddenly, things that never made sense before started clicking into place. The people failing on Kickstarter? They were Forests trying to market like Tundras. The authors with tiny lists but giant launches? Aquatics who'd built loyal superfans across fragmented platforms. The ones who couldn't finish a book? Tundras stuck without a launch to aim for. Deserts trying to act like Grasslands. Grasslands trying to act like Deserts.

We saw it everywhere.

The publishing industry has long been dominated by authors who write fast, ride trends, and optimize for volume and profit. That model works. It works really well, especially in places like Kindle Unlimited and ghostwriting, but it's not the *only* way to succeed and it's not the right fit for most creatives.

Right now, we're watching a shift in the landscape. Platforms like Substack, Kickstarter, and Beventi are blowing open the doors for other types of creators to thrive on their own terms.

What used to be a one-size-fits-all game is now a multiverse.

We don't need you to be someone you're not. We just need you to understand how you work, and to build a system around that.

That's what *The Author Ecosystems* is about.

This book will help you identify your natural tendencies, avoid the burnout traps that come from misalignment, and make decisions that support your unique author career. You'll learn what platforms fit your strengths, what marketing styles feel effortless instead of exhausting, and how to scale your business without sacrificing your sanity.

We also walk you through the healthiest and unhealthiest habits of each type, how to work with collaborators across ecosystems (trust me, this is huge), and how to filter the mountain of writing advice out there through a lens that works for *you*.

We've pulled this framework across everything—from craft to sales funnels, Kickstarter to email marketing, convention sales to community building—and we keep refining it as the industry evolves.

At the core of it all is this:

You don't have to do it all. You just have to do what works for *your ecosystem.*

If you're tired of banging your head against strategies that feel like they work for everyone but you… you're in the right place.

This book isn't a rulebook. It's a map. One that helps you finally make sense of where you are, how you operate, and where you're meant to go next.

THE DESERT ECOSYSTEM

Fast. Focused. Ruthlessly Efficient.

Let's start with the ecosystem that's historically dominated the publishing landscape.

Deserts are survivors. Tactical, lean, highly adaptable. They thrive in resource-scarce environments by doing more with less. Their superpower is efficiency. Deserts look at an opportunity and ask, "How can I win *today*?" They don't need it to be sexy. They just need it to work.

In many ways, the Desert archetype became the industry default, especially with the rise of Kindle Unlimited, rapid release publishing, and ghostwriting. For a long time, it seemed like the only "real" way to succeed as an indie author was to pump out genre fiction on a rigid schedule, write to market, and feed the algorithm gods.

And it *can* work. Some of the most profitable authors we know are Deserts. They've built systems, dialed in their tropes, and scaled their catalogs into revenue machines.

But not everyone is built to be a Desert. If you're *not* a Desert and you try to force yourself into that model? You're going to break.

This ecosystem isn't about artistic depth or slow-burn community-building. It's about *execution*. About velocity. About being faster, leaner, and more data-driven than the competition.

Deserts aren't here to feel all the feelings. They're here to deliver product. Full stop.

TRAITS OF A DESERT

- **Speed-focused**: Deserts move fast. They don't need a perfect book. They need a book that *ships*.
- **Trend-aware**: They spot market gaps, hit rising genres, and drop content when the timing is right.
- **Tactically driven**: Everything is part of a system including writing, launching, advertising, scaling. It's all part of the engine.
- **Minimalist marketers**: Deserts don't spend months building community. They build a funnel, test the ads, and optimize for ROI.

- **Emotionally detached**: They don't romanticize the work. They produce. If the market doesn't respond, they move on.

WHAT SUCCESS LOOKS LIKE FOR DESERTS

A healthy Desert has systems for everything: outlining, drafting, editing, cover design, blurb writing, publishing, promotion. They know their tropes, their readers, their competitors. Their work is dialed in to hit genre expectations *on purpose*. They track data, tweak quickly, and test ruthlessly.

Their marketing is lean. Think low-cost reader magnets, Facebook ads, newsletter swaps, backlist optimization. They're masters of sales funnels and "90-day cliffs".

When everything is working, Deserts generate steady cash flow. They may not have a huge audience, but the audience they *do* have is highly targeted. They're not building community, they're building income.

WHERE DESERTS STRUGGLE

Burnout is the big one. Deserts can run hot, especially when chasing trends or trying to match the pace of others in their niche. Because they're constantly producing and rarely pausing to refill the creative well, they risk hitting a wall and wondering, "Why do I even *like* this anymore?"

There's also the risk of commodification. When you're producing fast and marketing to data, it's easy to lose touch with *why* you started writing in the first place. That's when creative stagnation sets in—and suddenly the money machine starts sputtering.

Plus, not every Desert author is ready to *scale*. A lot of new writers try to become Deserts without the infrastructure. They don't have processes, editors, ad budgets, or audience insight. They crash hard trying to keep up with publishing models built by people five years and twenty books ahead of them.

BEST PLATFORMS AND STRATEGIES FOR DESERTS

Deserts thrive on systems where speed and scale are rewarded. That includes:

- **Kindle Unlimited (KU)**: Short-term sales windows, rapid release, and voracious genre readers? Check.
- **Amazon Ads and Facebook Ads**: Great for pushing books in a tested series.
- **BookFunnel and StoryOrigin**: For building lead magnets and list swaps at scale (*not for community building*).
- **Serialized platforms**: If you can produce consistently and meet deadlines.
- **Rapid-release series and pen names**: Build it, launch it, rinse, repeat.

Deserts also work well in ghostwriting, content writing, and freelance fiction where deadlines matter more than personal voice.

The Desert model isn't *bad*. It's just not for everyone.

If you're a Desert, lean into it. Build the machine. Find your rhythm. Automate everything you can. But remember:

it's okay to slow down once in a while. Even Deserts get rain occasionally.

If you're not a Desert, stop trying to be one. There are other ways to win.

You don't have to outpace everyone. You just have to build a system that works for *you*.

THE GRASSLAND ECOSYSTEM

Slow. Strategic. Built to Last.

Grasslands don't look flashy at first glance. They're not swinging from launch to launch or chasing trends like Deserts. They're not pouring their soul into serialized chapters or building immersive fandoms like Forests or Aquatics. And yet, when you look a little closer you'll find that some of the most stable, sustainable, and quietly profitable author businesses out there are built by Grasslands.

These authors aren't trying to win the short game. They're planting roots.

Grasslands are thinkers, planners, builders. They don't just write a book; they build a *body of work*. They write strategically, often obsessively, around one central idea, genre, theme, or worldview. Their power comes from depth, consistency, and a clear sense of their lane.

If Deserts win by shipping fast, Grasslands win by becoming *undeniable* over time. They're the ones who create definitive guides, cornerstone series, and content ecosystems that compound year after year.

A healthy Grassland can spend ten years talking about the same topic from a thousand different angles and still feel energized by it. Their joy isn't in the pivot; it's in the *iteration*.

TRAITS OF A GRASSLAND

- **Evergreen-minded**: Grasslands love content that holds value over time. They're in it for the long haul.
- **Focused on mastery**: Rather than hopping between genres, they go deep into one niche until they become a known expert or voice.
- **Consistency-driven**: They prefer sustainable habits to sprints. Give them a solid routine, and they'll thrive.
- **Big-picture thinkers**: Grasslands often have a larger mission, brand, or thesis behind their work.
- **Reluctant to launch**: They sometimes struggle with perfectionism and "not ready yet" syndrome.

Grasslands often overlap with nonfiction authors, long-form content creators, and serial educators. If you've ever said, "I just want to help people understand this one thing," you might be a Grassland.

WHAT SUCCESS LOOKS LIKE FOR GRASSLANDS

At their best, Grasslands are slow-burning powerhouses. They create high-value content and show up consistently over time. Their launches aren't always flashy, but they're reliable. Their sales may not spike, but they compound.

Grasslands often build the kind of backlist that pays dividends for years. They're great at SEO, discoverability, and repurposing content in new ways. Their social media may look quiet, but behind the scenes they're building libraries, frameworks, and long-term assets.

They tend to do exceptionally well with:

- Evergreen nonfiction
- Practical how-to guides
- Series with lots of books and a rich, deep lore.
- Email marketing and Substack
- Long-term planning and business infrastructure

They're also great collaborators, because they understand how to bring value into systems that already exist.

WHERE GRASSLANDS STRUGGLE

The biggest Grassland trap? **Over-preparing.**

Grasslands have high standards. That's a gift, but it also means they often delay launching. They keep refining, researching, revising. They start new content plans instead of finishing the current one. They want every blog post, newsletter, or book to be airtight, and that perfectionism can kill momentum.

Another challenge? Visibility. Grasslands are builders, not performers. They don't usually love being the face of a brand. So, unless they build strategic partnerships or strong SEO pipelines, their work can go unnoticed, even when it's excellent.

They also burn out when forced to operate at sprint speeds. If they try to run like a Tundra or Desert—rapid launching, fast publishing—they usually crash hard. Grasslands need time and space to thrive. If the ecosystem they're in doesn't give them that, they'll wither.

BEST PLATFORMS AND STRATEGIES FOR GRASSLANDS

Grasslands thrive in systems that reward depth, reliability, and cumulative value. That means:

- **Substack and Email Newsletters**: Perfect for slowly building trust and showcasing expertise.
- **Courses & Workshops**: Especially evergreen offers that can be reused and resold.
- **SEO Blogging**: Grasslands can dominate long-tail keyword traffic.
- **Podcasting & YouTube**: When planned strategically, these channels become legacy content.
- **Wide publishing**: When paired with high-quality, genre-consistent backlists.

They often do better outside of fast-paced launch cultures like Kickstarter unless paired with a Tundra-style partner who can run point on urgency and momentum.

Grasslands build quietly. They grow in layers. But once their ecosystem is in place? It's incredibly hard to uproot.

We see a lot of Grasslands who think they're broken because they're not launching fast enough or selling on emotion or growing their TikTok audience by dancing in cosplay.

You're not broken. You're just not a Forest or a Tundra or an Aquatic. You're a builder. A teacher. A system-maker.

You don't need to dominate the charts today. You just need to show up consistently enough that your body of work becomes too valuable to ignore.

That's how Grasslands win.

THE TUNDRA ECOSYSTEM

Explosive. Cyclical. Launch-Oriented.

Tundras aren't here to write forever. They're here to write *for something*. They don't just create, they *build toward*. If there's no deadline, no audience waiting, no ticking clock pushing them forward, they often freeze up, but give them a big launch, a hard date, and a shot to make noise? They light up like fireworks.

Tundras are the sprinters of the author world.

They don't do well with never-ending content calendars or slow-drip marketing. They need a build-up. A release. A moment to explode. Their energy is cyclical, vacillating between intense and all-consuming during the push, followed by a necessary period of rest and recovery.

If you've ever crushed a Kickstarter then ghosted your audience for three months? You might be a Tundra. If your productivity spikes the moment you set a public launch date, and completely dies when you're "just working on the next thing"? Welcome to the ice fields.

Tundras don't create for the sake of it. They create for *impact*.

TRAITS OF A TUNDRA

- **Launch-driven**: Deadlines, campaigns, and events are what get them moving.
- **Hype-loving**: They enjoy the energy of anticipation— teasing a new project, revealing covers, running countdowns.
- **Focused creators**: When they're in a production sprint, they can be unstoppable.
- **Recovery-based**: After a big push, they *have* to rest. Otherwise, they burn out (*and so does your audience*)
- **Emotionally invested**: Their launches feel personal. Wins are euphoric. Losses can knock them out.

Tundras often show up as indie novelists, comic creators, crowdfunding experts, and launch-focused marketers. They're not usually the ones emailing every Tuesday. But when they hit your inbox? *It's with a mission.*

WHAT SUCCESS LOOKS LIKE FOR TUNDRAS

A healthy Tundra is a launch machine.

They plan their calendar around campaign cycles. They stack content and production schedules to align with big releases. They know how to build buzz, how to galvanize a list, and how to create momentum. Tundras excel in event-based marketing: Kickstarter, convention signings, limited-edition drops, box sets, timed bonuses.

They don't need a massive audience, just a motivated one. Their strength isn't in being everywhere, it's in showing up *exactly when it counts*, with energy that's contagious and stakes that feel real.

And when the launch is over? They disappear to the mountains (figuratively…*usually*) to recharge and gear up for the next one.

Tundras don't win by being always-on. They win by knowing when to turn it on and when to turn it *off*.

WHERE TUNDRAS STRUGGLE

Tundras are masters of momentum… but can be total messes without it.

They often struggle with consistency. If there's no urgency, no countdown, no audience to perform for, they drift. They'll second-guess their work, overthink every chapter, or jump to a new project just to get that dopamine hit of "starting fresh."

Burnout is real, and it's brutal. Their cycles are intense, so Tundras are prone to flaming out, especially if they try to go back-to-back-to-back without building in recovery time.

Another trap? The Launch Spiral.

This happens when a Tundra finishes a project and immediately feels the need to start hyping something else *even if the last launch nearly killed them*. They don't know how to rest without guilt, so they overcommit and self-sabotage.

Unhealthy Tundras also risk tying their self-worth to launch outcomes. If a campaign flops or underperforms, it doesn't just feel like a business failure, it feels *personal*, and that can cause deep creative paralysis.

BEST PLATFORMS AND STRATEGIES FOR TUNDRAS

Tundras thrive where visibility spikes, deadlines matter, and launches have built-in urgency. Their best playgrounds include:

- **Kickstarter & Crowdfunding**: The ultimate Tundra environment, fixed deadlines, public stakes, and community buzz.
- **Limited-time launches**: Box sets, pre-order campaigns, bundles with bonuses.
- **Convention Sales**: High-energy, face-to-face selling with built-in adrenaline.
- **Email Marketing (bursts)**: Not daily newsletters, but strategic, time-based campaigns around launches.
- **Pre-order windows**: Give them something to build hype around.

Tundras can also do well with seasonal schedules with 3–4 big pushes per year, spaced out with strategic downtime. They don't need to be *everywhere*. They need to be *where it matters*, when it matters most.

Tundras are volcanic. Cold most of the time, until they erupt with creative fire.

If that's you, embrace it. Don't beat yourself up for not being consistent. Be *cyclical* on purpose. Plan your year around your bursts. Build rest into your schedule like it's sacred.

You're not lazy. You're just hibernating until it's launch season.

Don't try to be "on" all the time. You're not built for it. You're not supposed to be. And when you try to be like a Desert or a Grassland, you're only accelerating your burnout.

Launch hard. Recover harder. That's the Tundra way.

THE FOREST ECOSYSTEM

Rooted. Resonant. Community-Centered.

If you're a Forest, your work isn't just about the stories you tell, it's about the *connection* you build with your audience through those stories. Forest authors don't want to just sell books; they want to be *seen*, to make readers feel *seen*, and to create something that feels like home for the people who find them.

That's the core of the Forest ecosystem: *belonging*.

These authors build careers on emotional resonance and authentic relationships. Their marketing isn't about chasing trends or running data-driven funnels. It's about trust. Identity. Vulnerability. When Forests are healthy, they build beautiful, tight-knit communities of superfans who buy every book, back every campaign, and recommend them endlessly, not because of a slick pitch, but because of the way the work *feels*.

Forests don't need a massive audience. They just need the *right* one.

TRAITS OF A FOREST

- **Brand-first thinkers**: Forests are often their brand. Their voice, aesthetic, and story all reflect who they are.
- **Emotionally tuned in**: They write from the heart and value deep emotional impact over high-concept spectacle.
- **Community-driven**: Forests thrive on relationships, both online and in person. They want conversation, not broadcast.
- **Shared language**: They build connection through giving people the shared language to communicate with each other.
- **Sensitive to rejection**: Forests take feedback (especially silence) *personally*—sometimes painfully so.

If you've ever said, "I want to write things that matter to people," or "I want to create something that makes readers feel seen," you're probably a Forest (or at least embracing your inner Forest).

WHAT SUCCESS LOOKS LIKE FOR FORESTS

When Forests are thriving, they build ecosystems that *feel alive*. Their readers follow them from genre to genre. Their newsletters feel like letters from a friend. Their social media is warm, engaging, and unmistakably *them*.

They might not publish ten books a year or spend thousands on ads, but when they do put something out into the world, it sells because people trust them. People care about them. People *want* to support them.

A Forest might do three releases a year. Or one. But they build loyalty that can last a lifetime.

Forests tend to do well with:

- Serialized fiction on Ream, Patreon, or Vella
- Crowdfunded book boxes or special editions
- Personal blogs or Substacks with strong author voice
- Convention appearances and live events
- Reader communities on Discord, Facebook, or Slack

They're also more likely to get fan art, emotional DMs, and unsolicited long emails thanking them for helping someone through a hard time.

WHERE FORESTS STRUGGLE

The downside of being a Forest? *Emotional exhaustion.*

Forests are deeply tied to their work. When things go well, they soar. But when a launch underperforms, when social media is quiet, when nobody replies to the newsletter they spent hours writing, they spiral.

Because Forests blur the line between personal and professional, every "no" feels like a rejection of *them.* That's dangerous. It can lead to long dry spells, imposter syndrome, and burnout.

They also have a hard time setting boundaries. They want to help everyone. They feel guilty charging money. They say yes too often, and they don't want to turn anyone off, even if they *want* to hear from them. So they avoid it. Or they force it and feel fake.

If Forests don't learn to protect their energy and filter feedback wisely, they'll eventually shut down altogether.

BEST PLATFORMS AND STRATEGIES FOR FORESTS

Forests do best where authenticity, story, and relationship-building are rewarded. That includes:

- **Patreon or Ream**: Monthly support from your most loyal fans in exchange for early access, bonus content, or behind-the-scenes insight.
- **Email newsletters with voice**: Not templated, automated drip sequences. Real emails. Stories. Invitations to connect.
- **Substack**: Especially powerful when paired with personal essays or serialized work.
- **Live events & reader groups**: Forests thrive in real-time connection, whether at a booth or in a comment thread.
- **Social platforms with high engagement**: Like Instagram stories, TikTok, or even YouTube when used for "day-in-the-life" content.

Forests don't need to be viral. They just need to be *consistent*. Show up. Be real. Let people in. That's your superpower.

You don't have to out-market anyone. You don't need to trick readers with scarcity or shout louder than everyone else. You need to *connect*.

You already know how to do that. You've probably been doing it for years without realizing it.

The key is to build your author business in a way that feels good *and* sustains you. That means setting boundaries. Saying no. Charging fairly. And remembering that silence is not always rejection. It's just the internet being the internet.

You're not here to be famous. You're here to be *felt*. Lean into that.

THE AQUATIC ECOSYSTEM

Expansive. Immersive. Multi-Platform Thinkers.

Aquatics don't just write books. They build worlds.

They're not looking to drop a one-off novel or even just a series. They want to create an *experience*. One that spans across formats, platforms, and mediums. Books become games. Characters become merchandise. Stories become lore-rich universes. And their audience? It's not just "readers", it's a *fandom*.

Aquatics are natural brand-builders. They think in terms of systems, ecosystems, multimedia extensions, and long-term intellectual property (IP) play. If they had unlimited resources, they'd turn their stories into full-blown franchises spanning books, board games, podcasts, music, art, animated shows, fan clubs, conventions, live readings, and who knows what else.

They are visionaries, but that vision comes with a cost.

Aquatics can see *everything*, but they struggle to focus on *one* thing at a time. Their creativity is sprawling. Their ideas multiply like sea foam. And unless they build the right infrastructure, they risk getting lost in their own oceans.

Still, when healthy, Aquatics can build publishing careers that stretch far beyond the bookshelf. They're not just authors; they're empires in motion.

TRAITS OF AN AQUATIC

- **Brand-centric**: Aquatics see themselves as creators of a *universe*, not just writers of books.
- **Multi-format minded**: They think in multimedia—comics, cards, courses, podcasts, merchandise, and beyond.
- **Systemic planners**: They love frameworks, lore bibles, interlocking arcs, and big-picture strategies.
- **Collaboration driven**: In order to build their universe, they are constantly collaborating with other brands who can introduce them to new audiences and validate their ideas.
- **Easily overwhelmed**: With so many ideas, execution becomes the bottleneck.

If you've ever said, "This isn't just a book, it's a *world people can live in*," or "I have ten projects in progress and can't pick which one to finish," you're probably an Aquatic.

WHAT SUCCESS LOOKS LIKE FOR AQUATICS

When they're in sync, Aquatics are unstoppable.

They build rich, multidimensional brands that capture attention across different channels. They might serialize part of their story on Substack, run a companion podcast, offer exclusive merch to subscribers, and crowdfund special editions or game expansions.

They do well with:

- Collaborations with other brands that can validate their work to new fans.
- Cross-media campaigns (book + comic + soundtrack + more)
- Immersive Kickstarter campaigns with layered reward tiers
- Subscriptions with fan club tiers (Patreon, Ream, etc.)
- Personal websites with stores, lore databases, and unique reader experiences

Aquatics can draw superfans who don't just read their books, they *inhabit* their worlds. When everything is aligned, these authors create ecosystems so magnetic that readers return again and again just to stay connected.

Aquatics thrive when they feel free to explore and expand—*as long as* they have structure to keep them grounded.

WHERE AQUATICS STRUGGLE

The danger of being an Aquatic? *Overextension.*

Aquatics often chase every idea that floats by. They start fifteen projects at once, try to be on ten platforms simultaneously, and constantly reinvent their strategy mid-launch. They say yes to too much. They burn through their budget, time, and energy trying to "do it all."

Because they have such a big vision, they often struggle with clarity. They confuse their audience (and themselves) with mixed messaging. They try to launch too many things at once. They delay projects because they're "not perfect yet." Their to-do list is infinite, and their follow-through can fall apart.

Another challenge? Team-building. Aquatics often *need* collaborators to execute on their vision—but resist giving up control. That leads to bottlenecks, burnout, and disappointment.

An unhealthy Aquatic can spin for years in the sea of ideas, drifting from project to project without ever finishing the boat that would take them to shore.

BEST PLATFORMS AND STRATEGIES FOR AQUATICS

Aquatics do best when they build a *universe* and invite people into it. That includes:

- **Kickstarter and crowdfunding**: Perfect for big, bold campaigns with physical rewards, stretch goals, and immersive experience design.

- **Direct sales (via Shopify, Payhip, WooCommerce)**: They can create full product lines, bundles, special editions, and upsells.
- **Substack or Patreon**: For serialized work, behind-the-scenes content, and layered community access.
- **Email lists (with segmenting)**: Aquatics often have multiple entry points into their brand, so custom funnels are powerful.
- **World-building websites**: With lore, timelines, maps, wikis, and interactive components.

The trick is: Aquatics must *prioritize* and *sequence*. Everything is possible, but not all at once. The ecosystem only thrives when the water is clear.

You're not broken for thinking big. The industry needs your vision. The readers want your worlds. But you have to *finish* something.

Don't try to launch three Kickstarters and a podcast in the same month. Don't over-promise and under-deliver. Don't try to act like a Desert or a Tundra because you feel behind.

You are an architect of imagination. You *build entire realities*. That's your gift. Just make sure you're building a bridge, not a maze.

And most of all? Find your rhythm. Get help. Ship something. Then grow from there.

You don't have to go viral. You just have to go *deep*—and bring your people with you.

EMBRACE YOUR WILD

Now you've seen the terrain. You've walked through deserts, hiked grasslands, weathered tundras, explored forests, and swum through deep waters. Maybe you saw yourself in one ecosystem. Maybe in two. Maybe you felt called out by all five.

That's okay.

This isn't about boxing yourself in. It's about **recognizing your natural patterns** so you can finally stop fighting yourself. Most of us spend years trying to market like someone we admire, only to burn out, stall out, or collapse under the weight of something that was never built for us in the first place.

You're not lazy. You're not broken. You're not failing because you suck at business. You're just using a map that wasn't drawn for your terrain.

The Author Ecosystems model exists to help you draw *your* map.

It gives you permission to stop trying to be a Desert if you're actually a Forest. To stop apologizing for your Grassland pacing. To lean fully into your Tundra sprints or Aquatic vision. To finally understand *why* that launch worked or didn't. Why that platform felt natural or made your skin crawl.

You don't need to do everything. You need to do the things that work for *you*.

And when you do? You'll notice something incredible start to happen:

- Your energy returns.
- Your launches get easier.
- Your writing feels joyful again.
- Your audience begins to grow, not because you're hustling harder, but because you're showing up *honestly*.

This isn't a straight line. Ecosystems evolve. You'll grow. You'll blend. You'll borrow tactics across types. That's normal. Many authors live on the edge between two ecosystems. Some evolve into another entirely as their careers expand.

The key is to **recognize your core tendencies** and build from there. If you try to scale your business from someone else's strengths, you'll collapse every time. But if you build on your *own* ecosystem—one rooted in your values, your pace, your skills—you'll grow something that lasts.

And it'll actually feel good.

You just needed permission to believe it could work, but if you want it anyway, then this is your permission.

Build your stack. Trust your pace. Embrace your weird. **You're not lost. You just needed a better map.**

Let's go build something beautiful.

CHAPTER 1

THE DESERT ECOSYSTEM

Efficiency as a Strategy

You've probably heard this story: Author goes from zero to six figures in less than a year. They publish a book every six weeks. They dominate a single genre. They optimize for Kindle Unlimited, stack ads with precision, and rake in page reads like clockwork. They don't just write fast—they *win fast*.

That author is usually a Desert.

And for a long time, they were held up as the gold standard for indie success. Maybe they still are. The author-as-machine. Crank out content, feed the beast, live off the algorithm. Deserts became the template everyone else was told to copy.

If you're not a Desert, trying to act like one will destroy you. And even if you *are* a Desert, staying healthy in this ecosystem takes more than hustle and spreadsheets.

Because Deserts? They burn hot. And they burn out just as fast.

What makes them powerful is the same thing that makes them vulnerable. They treat books like products and themselves like a factory.

That's not a flaw, it's a strategy. However, it only works when the machine behind it is tight, tuned, and sustainable. Otherwise, everything dries up.

This chapter is your guide to being a *smart* Desert. The kind that lasts.

THE DESERT IDENTITY

Deserts are lean, fast, and focused. They operate like businesses from day one. No romanticism. No hand-wringing over inspiration. Deserts don't need a muse; they need a *plan*.

Once they see a hole in the market, they jump into action to fill it, and they fill it with their whole self.

They thrive in environments where speed and efficiency are rewarded. Deserts don't mind writing to trend. They *prefer* it. They get bored easily, pivot fast, and don't get too emotionally attached to a single book, series, or brand.

They're not in this to "make art". They're in it to make money *doing something they love,* and they'll build whatever system works to make that happen.

Common Desert beliefs include:

- "Done is better than perfect."
- "If it's not selling, I move on."
- "The next book will fix it."

They trust the numbers. They trust the schedule. They trust the machine.

And when it works, it really, really works.

When it comes to creating products, their goal is to make the perfect representation of a genre, one that will perfectly satisfy as many readers as possible.

While other ecosystems rely on siphoning off a portion of the market, Deserts are interested in writing books that please the whole market, which is both a blessing and a curse.

HOW DESERTS WIN

A healthy Desert is like a solar panel in the middle of a wide-open landscape; self-sufficient, focused, and optimized.

They know their genre. They know what's hot. They know what sells. And they write directly into that lane. They don't spend six months wondering if the idea is "good enough." They build a production schedule, outline the book, and get it written.

Their publishing system is dialed in:

- Covers are genre-accurate.
- Blurbs are algorithm-tuned.
- Launch strategy is rinse-and-repeat.
- Ad funnels are already running by launch day.

Deserts build book catalogs like architects:

- Rapid-release trilogies.
- Shared-world series.

- Pseudonyms stacked for multiple subgenres.

They often make their money not off long series, but off moving genres and writing styles to match where the market is *right now*. Not in three months, six months, or two years, and they don't care about evergreen tropes.

They want to hit the market this minute, which is amazing, but also…

DESERT PITFALLS

…there's a catch.

Deserts publish *a lot*, but because they bounce from idea to idea, series to series, trend to trend, very few of those books have staying power. Their catalog might look huge, but it's usually made up of half-finished arcs, short-lived niches, and ghosted audiences.

When they look back at their catalog they realize they don't really have one. They have a bunch of books that sound and read different from each other, and have no consistency that builds long-term readers.

Additionally, writing to market means following the market down rabbit holes they might not want to go, and when that happens, the books start to feel flat. Maybe authors make 50% or more of their income on backlist, and while Deserts burn fast and burn hot, they also burn out. When they do, they find they don't have as much to show for it as they should.

Their system works well—until it doesn't.

Common Desert pitfalls include:

- **Burnout**: Output is everything. Rest isn't baked in.
- **Catalog bloat**: 15+ books, no flagship series. Nothing evergreen.
- **Shallow reader connection**: Fans read a book, then forget the author's name.
- **Platform dependency**: One algorithm shift and income evaporates.
- **Creative emptiness**: Writing starts to feel like assembly-line work.

Deserts are great at launching but bad at nurturing. And without a plan to support backlist titles, the money dies when the machine slows down.

WHAT DESERTS NEED TO STAY HEALTHY

Deserts are built to survive in harsh conditions, but just because you *can* push endlessly doesn't mean you *should*. If you're going to keep your system sustainable (and yourself sane), you need more than optimization. You need maintenance.

This section isn't about slowing down for the sake of it. It's about running smart. About building a creative machine that works without grinding your spirit into dust.

1. FIND YOUR FOREVER PACE

There's a pace you could write at *forever* with energy, joy, and consistency. That pace isn't frantic. It's not about "writing all the words." It's about writing the *right* amount consistently, so you don't flame out.

Ask yourself:

- *What's the amount of writing I can sustain without stress, guilt, or resentment?*
- *What's the life I'd want to live if I never got famous, but always stayed steady?*

That's your **forever pace.** And if you build your system around that—not the pace of Facebook groups or KU legends—you can write for the rest of your life.

Build your life to protect that rhythm:

- Structure work sprints around your peak hours.
- Create guardrails (word count minimums and maximums).
- Block time for rest *before* you burn out.
- Let seasons of intensity be followed by seasons of stillness.

Deserts don't die from heat. They die from depletion.

2. CREATIVE RECOVERY = STRATEGIC NECESSITY

Burnout isn't a sign of weakness. It's the natural byproduct of output without replenishment. Build recovery into your process on purpose.

- Take every fourth month off from drafting.
- Block "clean" weeks after launches where no writing or promotion happens.
- Schedule one project per year that's just for *you*—a passion project, experiment, or genre palate cleanser.

Reminder: Your pace is a tool. Not a personality.

3. NURTURE, DON'T JUST LAUNCH

Deserts tend to push a book and move on, but your backlist is full of value if you actually promote it.

Tactics that keep the backlist alive:

- Create promo schedules: cycle old titles through newsletter swaps and ad pushes.
- Bundle backlist books into box sets or omnibuses.
- Add BookFunnel/Payhip direct sale bundles with bonuses.
- Periodically update covers or blurbs to match current genre trends.

The catalog doesn't need to be big—it needs to be *active*.

4. CHOOSE PILLAR PROJECTS TO CULTIVATE

You don't have to treat every book equally. Pick one or two titles (or series) to invest in over time.

That might mean:

- Adding a hardcover edition.
- Doing a collector's print run.
- Turning it into audio, a graphic novel, or serialized content.
- Writing a spinoff novella, character prequel, or short story tie-in.

Deserts excel at speed, but sometimes slowing down on the right title can yield long-term ROI.

5. KEEP A TIGHT STACK

Don't try to build a business off 15 different tactics. Your stack should be simple, clear, and tuned to your ecosystem.

The core Desert stack often looks like:

- KU or genre-targeted Amazon strategy
- Reader magnet + onboarding funnel
- Amazon + Facebook ads optimized to Book 1 of a series
- Launch-focused writing schedule (every 6–10 weeks)
- Evergreen backlist marketing

That's enough. You don't need a podcast, TikTok, YouTube channel, and 10 pen names. Simplicity keeps the system sustainable.

6. DIVERSIFY—INTENTIONALLY

Eventually, the market will change. KU will shift. Ads will spike. Reader behavior will evolve. Deserts need contingency plans. Ways to diversify without losing focus:

- Build an email list that's *yours,* off Amazon, off social.

- Create a direct sales store for bundles, box sets, or bonus editions.

- Expand one successful series into a passion project; launch on Kickstarter, serialize it, or do a special edition.

Don't diversify *randomly*. Build from what's working. Expand **outward**, not sideways.

BUILD YOUR DESERT STACK

Here's the good news: if you're a Desert, the road is clear. You don't need to guess. You need to build a system that maximizes what you're already good at—speed, structure, and scale—and eliminate everything that slows you down.

Use this as your starter blueprint.

STEP 1: PICK YOUR PROFIT PATH

Choose a **high-readthrough niche** in KU or a genre with strong sales data.

- Research Amazon's top 100 in your chosen category.
- Analyze the tropes, length, pacing, covers, and blurbs.
- Decide: one genre, one tone, one goal.

Don't reinvent the wheel. Just aim it in the right direction.

STEP 2: PLAN A 6-BOOK RELEASE CADENCE

You don't need ten books. You need one series with six strong entries, broken up into two trilogies. Deserts know the perfect series is six books, with a massive drop-off in readership at book seven, so they plan two trilogies, which gives them two box sets and one six book omnibus.

After that, they are often off to the next thing. So, to make this work:

- Outline your two trilogies or shared-world series.
- Set release dates 4–8 weeks apart.

- Build a production schedule backward from your deadlines.
- Your job is to train the algorithm and the reader to expect regular drops.

STEP 3: BUILD YOUR FUNNEL

- Create a short prequel or side story as your **reader magnet**.
- Set up a **landing page** using BookFunnel or StoryOrigin.
- Create a **5-email onboarding sequence**:
  - Welcome + freebie
  - Introduction to your world
  - Author story or background
  - First pitch
  - Reminder + call to action

Automate it and let it run.

STEP 4: SET UP ADVERTISING

- Start simple: $5–$10/day Amazon Ads to Book 1.
- Track CTR, CPC, and readthrough over 30 days.
- Use FB Ads for launch bursts or wide testing.
- We're also trying to bump up your rank so that Amazon sees consistent sales.

The goal isn't volume at first, it's **data**. Refine as you go.

STEP 5: LAUNCH AND MONITOR

- Release each book cleanly and consistently.
- Stack promos: newsletter swaps, ad bursts, promo sites.

- Watch your readthrough data. That's your profit margin.
- After launch, cycle that book back into your rotation every 90–120 days.

STEP 6: OPTIMIZE OR EXPAND

- Create a box set or omnibus for the trilogy.
- Offer a direct bundle with exclusive extras.
- Test audio or short-run Kickstarter editions for your most loyal readers.

You don't need 20 books. You need 3 that earn their keep. Even the most successful authors know that only 20% of their books deliver 80% of their revenue.

SURVIVE AND SCALE INTELLIGENTLY

You don't need to work yourself into the ground to be a successful Desert.

In fact, the smartest Deserts are the ones who *don't* act like machines. They act like strategists. Engineers. Operators.

They know how to launch—but they also know how to rest. How to protect their energy. How to build systems that support the work without suffocating the joy.

Being a Desert isn't about writing fast, it's about **thinking clearly**.

It's knowing what to write, when to write it, and when to walk away.

And above all, it's about building a creative career that can **sustain itself without breaking you in the process.**

If that's your path, then this is your map. Go build your stack.

You've got this.

CHAPTER 2

THE GRASSLAND ECOSYSTEM

Owning the Conversation Through Depth

They didn't get famous overnight. They didn't spike a viral launch. But it feels like they've always been there. Every week. Every month. Every year.

Blogging. Emailing. Posting. Responding. Publishing.

If you type something into Google about their genre, *they* show up. If you ask a question on Reddit, *someone links their stuff*. If you wander onto Substack or Amazon or YouTube, there they are again. Not flashy. Not chasing the next big thing. Just… there. Always.

That's a Grassland. They don't win with speed or trend-hopping. They win with **presence**.

They show up so consistently, for so long, and with such comprehensive value that they become the *default voice* in the space. Their strength isn't virality, it's inevitability. They write evergreen content, build rich backlists, and create layered ecosystems that continue to pay off years after publication.

They don't just write books. They build *topic libraries*. They don't chase exposure. They **become the reference**. They don't just work in the system; they help build the system.

THE GRASSLAND IDENTITY

Grasslands are methodical, comprehensive, and relentless. They are not in a rush but they are always moving. They think in terms of systems, timelines, and content depth. They rarely go all-in on a single title. Instead, they build wide-reaching frameworks of interconnected work that generate long-term credibility and compounding returns.

Their currency isn't buzz, it's trust.

They often start slow, invisible, and underfunded. But over time, their consistency makes it impossible to ignore them. They build from a deep internal conviction: that **owning a topic** is more powerful than momentary relevance.

What makes Grasslands special is that they can predict where the market is going, and help influence the inevitability of it getting there. When they do, then they are the one everyone turns to when the time comes.

Common Grassland beliefs:

- "Every piece of content is a long-term asset."
- "I'm not building for today; I'm building for five years from now."
- "People may not notice now, but they'll *have* to notice eventually."

Where Deserts aim to dominate the sales charts today, Grasslands want to own the entire *category* tomorrow.

They write content that backlinks itself. They write for the most influential blogs. They create flywheels of trust and consistency. They don't burn fast, they *root deep*.

HOW GRASSLANDS WIN

When Grasslands thrive, they become institutions. They dominate SEO. They're cited in articles. They're bookmarked, shared, referenced, and recommended not because of hype, but because they are *reliable*.

A well-built Grassland platform often looks like:

- A **massive blog archive** with optimized SEO
- A **robust newsletter** with consistent open rates and evergreen sequences
- A **library of books** (nonfiction or fiction) that speak to a tightly defined reader
- **Cross-linked ecosystems** from books to courses to podcasts to social posts
- A backlog of content with **backlinks stacked for years**
- The most comprehensive collection of work on a topic

They often own niche keywords. They rank in search. Their funnels are long, slow, and sticky. They are:

- The author with 20 nonfiction books on variations of one topic.
- The blogger-turned-publisher who gets 50K hits/month on longform essays.
- The YouTuber who has reviewed every book in a genre and launches to a ready-made audience.
- The Substack writer who's published every Tuesday for three years, and can link 100+ essays in their archive.

Grasslands don't just write books; they build bodies of work. Their backlist *is* their engine.

And when readers find them, they stick around. Because there's always more.

WHERE GRASSLANDS STRUGGLE

Grasslands don't often crash, they stall. And that stall is deadly.

Because while they're great at building engines, they're often reluctant to drive them at full speed. They like doing a little bit of work every single day, instead of a ton of work at once.

They can spend years laying groundwork without ever fully capitalizing on it. They'll write blog post after blog post, build newsletter after newsletter, but hesitate when it's time to sell.

They also struggle with **decision paralysis**. With so much content to leverage, it's hard to know what to push, when, or how.

Common Grassland pitfalls:

- **Endless preparation**: Always researching, outlining, writing, never launching.
- **Under-promoting**: Belief that "great work will find its audience eventually."
- **Content sprawl**: Too many platforms, too many formats, no clear funnel.

- **List fatigue**: Weekly emails that deliver value but never ask for anything.
- **Platform risk**: Heavy reliance on Substack/Medium/SEO without true ownership.
- **Never asking for a sale**: Since monetization is a friction point that makes people turn away, and that is death for a Grassland, they never ask.

Worst of all, Grasslands can become **invisible experts**—trusted, respected, and *monetarily broke*.

GRASSLAND PITFALLS

Grasslands have never seen a problem they couldn't fix if they just thought about it perfectly or wrote about it in the right way, so they are constantly writing and researching, but never solving.

You don't just *have* a lot of content. You *create* a lot of content. Constantly. You've been writing essays for years, maintaining a weekly newsletter, producing books, building frameworks, and somehow, you still feel like you're behind.

That's the paradox of being a Grassland. You know more than most. You've published more than most. And yet, your ecosystem often feels like a content graveyard, so much depth, but no clear path through it. No obvious entry point. No pressure behind it.

You've created the library. But the door's unmarked.

Here's where it goes wrong:

- **Over-researching, under-launching**: Grasslands often wait until everything is "ready." But with content, *it's never ready*. That wait kills momentum and income.
- **Audience confusion**: When you've written 37 articles, 14 books, and 6 different newsletters, readers have no idea where to start.
- **Perfection paralysis**: You know what "good" looks like. So you freeze when something doesn't meet your own impossible standards.
- **Content fragmentation**: Some of your best work is buried 50 clicks deep on your blog or in a newsletter archive nobody opens.
- **No monetization path**: You've built trust but haven't made offers. You're an authority, but not a business.

And when burnout hits (yes, Grasslands burn out too), it's not from *not having ideas,* it's from drowning in them.

WHAT GRASSLANDS NEED TO STAY HEALTHY

The good news? You're not starting from scratch. You're not broken. You're just tangled.

Your path to success is about **clarity, not speed**. It's not about "more content", it's about aligning what you already have into something coherent, discoverable, and valuable.

Here's how to keep your ecosystem fertile.

1. CLARIFY YOUR CORE TOPIC (OR BRAND THESIS)

You can't be known for everything. Choose what you want to own. Ask:

- What am I writing *about,* really?
- What promise ties my blog, newsletter, books, and courses together?
- If someone found me today, what would they assume I'm "the expert" in?

That answer should show up on your website, email welcome sequence, book titles, and pinned posts. Otherwise, you're invisible.

2. CREATE A NAVIGATION LAYER

Most Grasslands don't need to *make more* content; they need to resurface what already exists. Start with:

- "Start Here" pages
- Topic hubs that organize blog posts or episodes
- Curated email sequences that teach a concept over time
- Backmatter that links to your best work, not just your next book

Don't leave it to readers to connect the dots. *Do it for them.*

3. ESTABLISH A PUBLISHING CADENCE YOU CAN SUSTAIN

You're a content machine. But machines need rhythm.

- Pick your baseline: 1 post/week, 1 email/week, 1 book/quarter.
- Use batching and automation to protect your creative energy.
- Schedule sprints for new projects *after* you've re-used what you already made.

- Leave room to resurface your backlist content.

This isn't about slowing down, it's about *not wasting what you've already built*.

4. PICK 1-2 CHANNELS TO DEEPEN

You don't need to be on every platform. Choose the ones that reward **depth over velocity**:

- Substack (with archives and sequences)
- A blog with proper SEO structure
- A podcast with evergreen episodes
- YouTube with bingeable tutorials

Depth is your weapon. Don't scatter it.

5. MAKE THE ASK—REPEATEDLY

Grasslands tend to assume their audience will "know" what to do next. They won't. Your content should always point somewhere:

- Buy this book.
- Join this sequence.
- Read this essay next.
- Hire me. Back me. Subscribe.

You've earned their trust. Don't squander it with ambiguity.

BUILD YOUR GRASSLAND STACK

Grasslands don't grow fast, but they *do* grow forever. You're not here for hype. You're here to build something *undeniable*. Something that earns trust, dominates your niche, and pays you long after the work is done.

That's what your stack is for.

This isn't just about staying healthy, it's about building a creative ecosystem with so much depth, connectivity, and value that it becomes the default destination for anyone who touches your topic.

Let's break that down.

1. CHOOSE A CORNER OF THE INTERNET TO OWN

Every great Grassland starts with a flag in the ground.

You don't need to own *everything*. You just need to own one idea, genre, niche, or question so thoroughly that when people go looking for answers, they find *you* over and over again. Ask:

- What have I written about more than anyone I know?
- What do people DM me about when they're stuck?
- What topic do I always circle back to, even when I try to leave it?

That's your anchor. Everything else grows from that seed.

2. TURN CONTENT INTO INFRASTRUCTURE

You've already made the content. Now build the roads between it. This means:

- Creating content paths ("If you liked this, read that.")
- Building hubs (topic landing pages, resource libraries)
- Grouping content by reader journey (beginner, intermediate, advanced)

Make it easy for someone to binge your work like Netflix. Don't make them dig through archives or type in keywords. *Guide them.*

3. STACK ASSETS IN PUBLIC

You don't need to go viral. You need to show your depth. Choose 1–2 channels where your *accumulated work* becomes obvious:

- A pinned Substack post linking your best essays.
- A YouTube playlist that walks through your key frameworks.
- A homepage that doesn't just "introduce you", it *proves* you.

Make your expertise visible. Not with noise, but with structure.

4. LADDER YOUR OFFERS

A Grassland thrives when your ecosystem leads somewhere.

Your blog leads to your book. Your book leads to your course. Your course leads to your community. Your community leads to your high-ticket offer.

Build your stack like a ladder:

- Each step gives value.
- Each step builds trust.
- Each step invites them *deeper into your ecosystem.*

Don't drop your audience into the ocean. Show them the shore, and how to walk there.

5. PRESERVE YOUR LEGACY

Grasslands are legacy ecosystems. You're building something that should still work 10 years from now.

So protect it:

- Own your domain and your email list.
- Keep backups of your work in case platforms fail.
- Revisit and update old content yearly.
- Build from frameworks, not fads.

Your work *should* be the Wikipedia of your niche. Your Substack *should* become a textbook. Your blog archive *should* outlive every new social platform that comes and goes.

That's the Grassland promise. Not to go fast, but to last.

THE QUIET POWER OF THE LONG GAME

Grasslands don't win by being loud. They win by being *everywhere*—quietly, steadily, perpetually.

You don't need a breakout moment. You need a clear voice and consistent rhythm. You don't need to chase the algorithm.

You need to build a system that lets your work compound over time. You've already written the pieces. You've already built half the library.

Now's the time to organize it, stack it, leverage it, and monetize it; not from scratch, but from the massive ecosystem you've already grown, one blog post, one email, one book at a time.

You don't need to chase the algorithm. The algorithm needs to catch up to *you*.

And once a Grassland becomes visible, *they don't fade again*.

So if you've ever felt behind because you're not loud enough, fast enough, or cool enough for the internet's shifting trends—stop. That's not your ecosystem.

You are not here to sprint. You are not here to shout. You are here to root, grow, and own the conversation.

And you're a lot closer than you think.

CHAPTER 3

THE TUNDRA ECOSYSTEM

Built to Launch

The book launch is coming. You've got the date circled. You're refreshing the pre-order page every five minutes. Your heart's racing. Your inbox is buzzing. You haven't eaten a vegetable in days.

And you have never felt so alive. That's Tundra energy.

Tundras don't thrive on slow, steady anything. They thrive on pressure. On momentum. On stakes. They need something to build toward. A moment. A peak. A deadline. Without that, they drift. But when it's go-time? They light up like a goddamn volcano under the snow.

They're cold for months, thinking, planning, building, and then, BOOM.

They launch.

That's not a bug. That's the system.

Where Deserts optimize, and Grasslands accumulate, Tundras **erupt**. They build intensity over time and then burn hot and fast during a launch cycle. And if they don't get that cycle? If there's no external countdown, no clear stakes, no public accountability?

They freeze. Hard. Tundras are the ecosystem of **explosive creativity**, timed perfectly.

And when they're healthy? They are *unmatched.*

THE TUNDRA IDENTITY

Tundras are event-based creators. They are cyclic. Rhythmic. Emotional. Focused.

They do their best work under deadline. They thrive when the stakes are real, when the audience is waiting, and when the project has a *point*. Without that, they stall out. They wander. They "sort of" write. They ghost their lists. They say they're planning, but they're really procrastinating because *there's no reason to finish yet.*

Once the gears click into place? Once the launch is scheduled? They become machines of momentum.

Common Tundra beliefs include:

- "If there's no deadline, I won't do it."
- "I just need to *announce* it to get started."
- "I work best under pressure."

Tundras aren't lazy. They're **latent**. They're snow-covered mountains with magma underneath.

Their creativity requires ignition. Once it's lit? Get out of the way.

HOW TUNDRAS WIN

Tundras win by turning every project into an event.

They understand drama. They understand narrative tension. They don't just publish, they build anticipation. They orchestrate campaigns. They engineer launches that feel like moments: Kickstarter countdowns, live reveals, cover drops, time-limited offers, high-ticket bundles.

When Tundras are healthy, they:

- Plan 2–4 big launches a year
- Build anticipation slowly, with pre-launch content
- Create immersive, high-stakes campaigns
- Deliver all-out during launch week—posts, emails, lives, bonuses, stretch goals
- Retreat afterward, recharge, and prepare for the next cycle

Tundras work especially well with:

- **Kickstarter** and crowdfunding (tight timelines + big drama = magic)
- **Live events and conventions** (they sell like monsters in person)
- **Product launches** (bundles, box sets, merch drops)
- **Seasonal sprints** (NaNoWriMo, challenge-based writing)

When they're firing on all cylinders, Tundras don't just *sell books*. They *create experiences*.

They pull in fans, collaborators, influencers, and new readers by building something *worth showing up for*. They make noise. They build buzz. And then they disappear into the ice until the next one.

WHERE TUNDRAS STRUGGLE

But let's be honest: when a Tundra doesn't have a launch? They vanish.

They feel lost, tired, unfocused. They keep "working" on things, but with no urgency. No real intention. They change covers. They start new drafts. They scroll instead of email. They over-edit. They get frustrated with their own lack of progress. But the truth is, they're not failing.

They're just **off-cycle**.

Core Tundra struggles include:

- **Inertia**: Without a deadline, they can't finish anything.
- **Post-launch crash**: Emotional collapse after a campaign ends.
- **Burnout masking as boredom**: They *think* they're lazy, but they're just depleted.
- **Over-promising**: Big launches with no recovery plan.
- **Ghosting their audience**: Going silent between events, losing momentum.
- **Launching too much**: Tundras need a cycle of launch, recover, build, and when they launch too much, they end up burning their audience and their money.

And worst of all? When they try to act like a Desert or a Grassland—when they try to be *consistent* or *quiet*—they break. Because Tundras aren't meant to be calm.

They're meant to **erupt on purpose**.

WHAT TUNDRAS NEED TO STAY HEALTHY

A Tundra doesn't need to create year-round. But they do need **cycles** with enough space to recover, reset, and reignite their creative drive.

Here's how they stay on track without burning to ash.

1. DESIGN YOUR LAUNCH CALENDAR LIKE A MARATHONER

You need peaks, but you also need valleys. Plan 2–4 launches per year and build your creative calendar around those bursts.

- 2 months: build-up and warm-up
- 1 month: launch prep and hype
- 2–3 weeks: launch execution
- 1 month: full recovery, no guilt

Set your launch dates first. Then plan backwards. That's how Tundras get things done.

2. CREATE A "DORMANT MODE" FOR OFF-CYCLE MONTHS

You don't need to vanish between launches.

Set up:

- A simple, evergreen email sequence that provides value and helps grow your audience.
- 2–3 blog posts or newsletters to rotate and reshare
- A lightweight content plan (like one post/month) that holds presence

This lets you disappear without losing visibility. These are your givebacks from your time of taking.

3. PRE-COMMIT PUBLICLY (WITH BOUNDARIES)

You get energy from *accountability*. Use it.

Announce your launch before it's ready. Lock in collaborators. Share the cover early. Make it real. But be careful not to over-promise. Always build recovery into your messaging.

Make this your mantra: *announce it to start, not to finish.*

4. TRACK ENERGY, NOT JUST OUTPUT

You don't need to be prolific. You need to be **charged**.

Check in weekly:

- Am I excited?
- Am I counting down or checked out?
- Is this sprint draining or fueling me?

If the answer is no, then pause. Recovery isn't a failure. It's part of your ecosystem.

BUILD YOUR TUNDRA STACK

The Tundra ecosystem isn't about constant output. It's about building a system that *anticipates the burst*—and has a plan for after the flame.

Here's your stack, stripped down and optimized.

STEP 1: LOCK IN YOUR LAUNCH CYCLE

Pick your rhythm: 2–3 launches per year. That's your pulse.

- Q1: new release or crowdfunding campaign
- Q2: rest and rebuild
- Q3: second launch or promo push
- Q4: planning season or a surprise drop

Tundras build *seasons*, not schedules.

STEP 2: DESIGN A LAUNCH THAT FEEDS YOU

Tundras don't just publish, they create moments.

- Kickstarter or crowdfunding (stretch goals, limited editions, campaign buzz)
- Convention appearances or book tours
- Themed box sets, merch drops, or bundles with time-based bonuses
- Pre-order campaigns with fan art, swag, and milestones
- Don't just launch a book. **Launch an event.**

STEP 3: BUILD A FLEXIBLE RECOVERY PLAN

You need a system that keeps you visible *without requiring constant attention.*

- Evergreen onboarding funnel for your email list
- Low-pressure content drip (e.g., one post or email a month)
- "Rest templates" that recycle past launches or content highlights

Make rest part of the system. Automate your off-season.

STEP 4: DEVELOP A HYPE ENGINE

You get your best work done when the spotlight's on. Use it.

- Tease the project 4–6 weeks before launch
- Do cover reveals, countdowns, live sessions
- Stack guest posts, podcast interviews, or influencer shares
- Create urgency: early bird pricing, limited inventory, countdown timers

Make people feel it's **now or never**. That's Tundra heat.

STEP 5: REBUILD DURING THE COOLDOWN

Use post-launch months to:

- Analyze what worked (and didn't)
- Reinvest profits into assets or ads
- Refuel your creative brain
- Outline the next campaign, but don't start it yet

Don't launch while empty. Let the pressure *build*.

STEP 6: REBUILD YOUR LIST LIKE YOUR CAREER DEPENDS ON IT (BECAUSE IT DOES)

After a launch, your list is **smoked**.

People unsubscribed. Others are tired of hearing from you. Some went dead quiet. And the truth is—your best buyers already bought.

That means if you want to launch again, you need *new blood*. Period.

Tundras can't coast on a tired list. You need a list that's primed, growing, and ready to blow when you light the fuse.

Here's how to rebuild between eruptions:

- **Create a new reader magnet** tied directly to your next launch or best series.
- **Run swaps or group promos** with authors in your genre. Not every week—just enough to bring in 200–500 new people per campaign.
- **Set up FB/IG lead ads** with a strong hook and a fast funnel.
- **Recycle launch content into evergreen onboarding**— turn your best emails into a 5-day welcome that builds trust and gets clicks.
- **Segment ruthlessly**: don't launch to your whole list. Launch to the *fresh* list.

Every Tundra launch depletes your audience. If you don't refill it, your next launch won't just underperform—it'll flop *hard*.

Tundras don't need a big list. But they **do** need a *responsive* one. And that means building it **again and again**. You can't launch on fumes. Refill the tank. Then light the match.

ERUPT ON PURPOSE

Tundras are not meant to be steady. They're meant to **explode, recover, and return stronger**.

So if you've ever felt broken because you can't be consistent, stop. You're not supposed to be. You're not a content engine. You're a campaign architect. A pressure-cooker of creative force.

You're not here to churn out endless posts. You're here to build *moments* that matter.

Moments people remember. Moments they gather around. Moments they back, fund, pre-order, and celebrate.

You burn hot, and then you freeze. That's okay. That's your power. Just make sure you give yourself the space to do both.

Don't try to be like the Grasslands with their constant content.
Don't try to be like Deserts with their never-ending pace.
Don't shame yourself for being quiet between launches.

Build a system that lets you erupt on purpose, and recover like you mean it.

Because when a Tundra launches right? Nobody else stands a chance.

CHAPTER 4

THE FOREST ECOSYSTEM

Build Belonging. Sell Identity.

This isn't just a book. It's a message. It's a mirror. It's a movement. It's something you *needed* to say.

You didn't write it for the algorithm. You didn't outline it from a market checklist. You wrote it because it *mattered* to you, and to the people you knew needed it most.

That's Forest energy. Forests don't publish books. They extend invitations to a world, a feeling, a voice, even a version of life that says, "You're not alone here."

Their work isn't just content. It's identity in motion. And their career isn't built on ads or scale or strategy. It's built on trust. Slow-earned. Deep-rooted. Soul-level connection.

Where Deserts optimize and Grasslands organize, Forests open themselves up.

They build bonds. They nurture community. They bring their whole self to the table and build brands that are inseparable from who they are.

When they're healthy? Forests create the kind of work that people tattoo on their bodies.

When they're not? They ghost, implode, or give away everything until there's nothing left.

THE FOREST IDENTITY

Forests are creators of intimacy. They are emotionally attuned, brand-driven, and community-minded. They don't just build platforms, they create *belonging*. Their readers don't just consume content. They form relationships with the work *and* with the creator behind it.

That emotional connection is their currency.

Common Forest beliefs:

- "I want my readers to feel seen."
- "Selling makes me nervous; I just want to connect."
- "I can't separate my work from who I am."

They don't just write a book. They live it. Forests naturally build audiences around:

- Deeply personal stories
- Vulnerable essays or newsletters
- Values-based fiction (grief, identity, hope, healing)
- Aesthetic branding that feels like *them*

They often overlap with memoirists, poets, literary fiction authors, serialized storytellers, and voice-driven content creators.

They win when they lean into emotional transparency + high-integrity marketing.

But it's a double-edged sword, because when your work *is* you it's really hard to take feedback, recover from failure, or ask for money without guilt.

HOW FORESTS WIN

Forests win through *resonance*. When their voice is aligned, when their values are clear, when their branding matches their story, then they attract the kind of fans who stick forever.

Forests don't need massive lists. They need **alignment**.

They do best with:

- **Serialized fiction or behind-the-scenes content** (Ream, Patreon, Substack)
- **Book boxes or special editions** with personal notes, signed copies, or gifts
- **A tightly knit reader community** (Discord, Facebook, Slack)
- **Values-first platforms** where people buy into a creator's story, not just the product

When Forests market well, it doesn't *feel* like marketing. It feels like sharing. Readers buy from them because they want to be close to the creator. They want to support the person, not just the project.

Forest strengths include:

- High engagement from a small audience
- Deep brand loyalty

- Powerful emotional conversion (people cry when they read your pitch, not because it's persuasive, but because it's real)
- A brand that expands with the author, not just the work
- Providing shared language that gives people the ability to communicate with each other.
- Making people feel seen in a way that they have to share it.
- Ambassador marketing wherein their community brings in new members of the community and amplifies your message.

Forests build careers with *slow intensity*. A thousand little emotional touchpoints, layered over time, which create **true fans**.

WHERE FORESTS STRUGGLE

But that same closeness? It's dangerous.

When your brand is *you*, rejection feels personal. When your audience expects vulnerability, showing up burned out feels impossible. And when you start writing what sells instead of what's real? You lose the magic, and you know it.

Common Forest traps include:

- **Emotional burnout**: Giving everything to your audience until there's nothing left for yourself
- **Boundary collapse**: Readers treat you like a friend, but you can't say no
- **Fear of selling**: You avoid making offers because you don't want to "exploit the connection"

- **Creative paralysis**: You stop writing because you're afraid it won't live up to what your audience expects
- **Imposter syndrome**: You confuse authenticity with oversharing and lose clarity in the process

Forests don't burn out from marketing. They burn out from mattering too much.

They tie their work to their identity. Their voice is their product. Their inbox is full of emotional disclosures and reader trauma-dumps. Their brand is built on *being present* all the time.

But they weren't built to carry all of that. And they certainly weren't built to carry it *alone*.

One of the biggest traps for Forests is thinking they need to be the center of their reader community. That they have to be the leader, the emotional support animal, the moderator, the content creator, the brand voice, the therapist, the hype machine, and the glue holding everything together.

But that's not their job. Forests don't need to *lead* the community. They need to nurture the connections between readers to give them the language, tone, stories, and emotional space to find each other.

That's what Forests are truly great at:

- Creating *shared identity*.
- Shared emotion.
- Shared worldview.

They are masters of ambassador marketing. When they're healthy, they build ecosystems where *fans do the work for them* by recommending the book, writing fanfic, making memes, sharing reels, or wearing the merch. The Forest just creates the story. The readers turn it into a movement.

But when a Forest tries to stay at the center of it all? They collapse.

Forest creators don't fail because they aren't talented. They fail because they're **exhausted** from trying to be everything for everyone.

Your job is not to be the sun.

Your job is to be the **soil** so your community can *grow itself.*

Forest creators don't disappear because they fail.
They disappear because they can't *sustain the intimacy they've built.*

WHAT FORESTS NEED TO STAY HEALTHY

You don't need to "harden up." You need to build systems that protect your heart. Forests will always feel more. That's your edge. But it has to be supported. Otherwise, you'll disappear every time a campaign underperforms or a fan crosses a line.

Here's how you build a Forest ecosystem that nourishes you:

1. DEFINE YOUR EMOTIONAL BOUNDARIES IN ADVANCE

Before you launch, before you post, before you hit publish, always define the line.

- What are you willing to share publicly?
- What's off-limits?
- What are your policies for reader DMs, feedback, access?

Boundaries aren't rejection. They're protection. For you *and* your readers.

2. WRITE YOUR "SAFE WORK" IN PARALLEL

Have one project that's just for *you*. Always. This might be:

- A series that doesn't sell but makes you feel alive
- A blog where you rant freely
- A sketchpad project you never publish

When everything you make is audience-facing, you lose the joy. Keep something sacred.

3. SEPARATE "SHARING" FROM "SERVING"

Not every newsletter has to be a diary. Not every post has to bare your soul. Build:

- Utility content (reader resources, character deep dives, fan extras)
- Community-led prompts (ask questions, let them talk for once)
- Curated content (what you're reading, watching, loving)

Balance the emotional labor. Don't bleed every week.

4. BUILD REVENUE INTO YOUR RELATIONSHIP

Don't make the sale an interruption. Make it a continuation of the relationship.

- Personal notes in your books
- Pre-orders that fund your next work
- Exclusive content that supports your income
- Subscriptions that blend community + access

If people love your work, they'll want to support you. But they have to know how. *And you have to let them.*

5. CREATE A "VISIBILITY TOOLKIT" FOR LOW-ENERGY WEEKS

Forests go dark when they're tired. But silence resets the trust clock.

Prepare for this by:

- Pre-writing 3–5 "low-spoon" newsletters you can send anytime
- Scheduling a quarterly "favorites" email with links to past work
- Automating a post-launch nurture sequence

Even when you're hiding, your forest can still grow.

BUILD YOUR FOREST STACK

Forests don't scale through force. They scale through **depth**. That means building a stack that supports emotional resonance *without requiring constant vulnerability.*

STEP 1: OWN YOUR STORY

Your brand is personal. But it still needs *structure.*

- Write your "about me" page like a manifesto
- Pin a story-based post or essay on your homepage
- Turn your origin story into a podcast episode, blog, or welcome sequence

You don't have to be everywhere. You just have to be authentically you *on purpose.*

STEP 2: CHOOSE 1-2 INTIMATE PLATFORMS

You don't need scale. You need connection. Great Forest platforms include:

- **Substack**: serials, essays, letters, community threads
- **Patreon/Ream**: behind-the-scenes content, serialized fiction, Q&A
- **Discord/Facebook**: for reader communities with strong moderation
- **Personal blog/newsletter**: curated content + storytelling + offers

Choose the ones that reward presence, not performance.

STEP 3: BLEND STORY + SALES

Forest readers support what they **feel connected to**. Sales strategies that work for you might include:

- Launch emails as love letters
- "Pay what you want" bundles
- Merch or books tied to personal moments
- Reader-sponsored writing time or stretch goals

If it's honest and clear, it's not pushy; it's powerful.

STEP 4: AUTOMATE TRUST

You don't have to be present every second to stay connected.

- Welcome sequences with your best writing
- Evergreen blog posts that link to offers
- Pre-scheduled check-ins during recovery months
- Content that resurfaces old wins ("here's what I made last year, and why it matters")

Forests thrive when their emotional labor is **structured, not spontaneous**.

STEP 5: PROTECT YOUR VOICE

You're the brand. You're the product. You're the relationship. So you have to **safeguard your capacity**. Build in:

- Recovery weeks after launches
- A quiet month every quarter
- A creative space where *nobody gets access but you*

When you protect your voice, it grows stronger. When you share it too thin, it disappears.

STEP 6: BUILD SHARED LANGUAGE INTO YOUR WRITING

Forest stories don't just entertain. They *name things* people couldn't explain before. They give readers the words to say:

"I've felt this. I *am* this. And now I finally have a way to talk about it."

That's the real magic of Forests' language. It's not a quote, it's a flag. When someone says it out loud, they're not quoting you. They're claiming themselves. They're sending a signal. They're saying: *"I need to find others like me."*

Your job as the writer isn't to craft slogans. It's to embed emotional truths into your stories that people recognize in themselves. Think:

- The quiet rebel who finally says, "I don't need to be loud to matter."
- The anxious teen who whispers, "We don't flinch."
- The woman who survived, and sees in your character the same survival.

These lines become TikTok trends, Discord role labels, tattoo inspiration, the way readers introduce themselves in your community, and give a shorthand for what it *feels like* to be part of your world

So don't just write for catharsis. Write for resonance. Create moments where your readers *see themselves clearly,* and then give them the language to tell the world who they are now.

That's how Forests scale. Not through outreach, but through *recognition.*

STEP 7: APPOINT AMBASSADORS AND INTENTIONAL ADVOCATES

You don't have to spread your message alone. In fact, you *can't.* Build a formal system for reader-powered growth:

- Recruit ARC readers and superfans intentionally
- Appoint community moderators, Discord leads, or forum coordinators
- Run ambassador programs with clear language, copy, links, and calls to action
- Offer private Q&As, early access, or exclusive swag for street team contributors

Let readers become the loudest voice in the room. Give them structure to do it well. This isn't "shout into the void" marketing. This is mission-based advocacy and nobody does it like a healthy Forest.

THE WORK THAT HOLDS PEOPLE

Forest authors don't change lives because they're the loudest. They change lives because they're the *most present.* Their readers feel held. Seen. Understood.

That's not a marketing trick. That's a gift, but it only works when it's given from a place of health, not exhaustion.

So if you've been told you're "too sensitive" to make it in publishing, or "too soft" to run a business, or "too emotionally attached" to sell your work?

That's not a flaw. That's your ecosystem.

You don't need a massive list. You don't need an ad budget. You don't need a launch calendar full of scarcity tactics.

You need space. You need protection. You need rhythm. You need trust.

Because Forests don't sell ideas. They sell identity. They sell **belonging**.

And when you get it right?

Your readers don't just buy your work. They *join your world*, and they *never want to leave*.

CHAPTER 5

THE AQUATIC ECOSYSTEM

Invent the System, Then Fill it

You didn't start by trying to be different. You tried to do it the "right" way. You followed the rules. Studied the market. Took the courses. You outlined your book. You picked a genre. You built the platform. You did everything they told you to do, and still, it didn't work.

Not because you didn't try hard enough, but because the system wasn't designed for the kind of work you create.

You didn't want to write what people already expected. You didn't want to sell the same story with a different name. You didn't want to grind your work down into something algorithmically convenient.

And once you saw how limiting the default model was, you couldn't unsee it. So you walked away.

Not to give up, but to build something better.

Your own thing in your own world where you own the rules.

Because you're not here to hack the machine. You're here to replace the machine with something more beautiful, immersive, and human.

That's Aquatic energy.

You don't write books. You build ecosystems. You don't iterate. You reinvent. And you're not just telling a story.

You're architecting a future. One that doesn't exist yet, but should.

THE AQUATIC IDENTITY

Aquatics are not content creators as much as visionary system architects.

Their stories don't live in a vacuum. They're interconnected, multi-layered, and cross-platform by design.

An Aquatic project is rarely "just a book." It's a:

- serialized narrative with interactive fan lore
- merch line built on in-world language and symbols
- deck-building game that teaches story logic
- soundtrack that captures emotional pacing
- blog archive, wiki, or podcast that expands the universe in real time

Every choice ties to the larger system. Every detail connects. Nothing is wasted.

Aquatics are driven by a compulsion to build cohesive, expansive, experiential brands. Not just IP, but *worlds you can live inside*.

Core Aquatic beliefs:

- "This doesn't exist yet, and it needs to."

- "If I can just get people to understand what I'm doing, they'll fall in love with it."
- "I can't build this inside the system. I have to make my own."

Aquatics aren't different on purpose. They're being honest about what the work demands, and the work demands something *entirely new*.

HOW AQUATICS WIN

Aquatics win by building immersive systems that can't be ignored.

Not better products. Better ecosystems.

They succeed when they:

- Invite others into a world, not just a story
- Create symbols, language, and lore that reward exploration
- Build emotional and intellectual trust over time, through depth and interconnectedness
- Deliver work so unique, it becomes impossible to compare or replicate

Aquatics don't scale through clarity. They scale through translation and validation.

Because the work is complex. The pitch is weird. The value doesn't fit neatly into a comp title or a 7-second elevator pitch.

So, they need collaborators and champions:

- A **Grassland** who can systemize the vision and organize the content into understandable lanes
- A **Tundra** who can take the complex idea and stage a dramatic, irresistible launch
- A **Desert** who can help turn one part of the world into a viable, sellable product

Aquatics don't just launch a book. They launch an entire paradigm shift.

And like all paradigm shifts, they hit resistance. Because people don't trust new systems right away.

That's why Aquatics need others to say:

- *"I know this seems different but I've used it, and it's brilliant."*
- *"I read the book. It's strange and beautiful and exactly what I needed."*
- *"You won't get it from the blurb, but once you're inside, you'll never want to leave."*

Aquatics win when other people give the reader permission to enter the world.

Once they're in?

They don't just follow. They build alongside you.

Because an Aquatic world is too big to hold alone, and the right readers don't want to be entertained. They want to *move in*.

WHERE AQUATICS STRUGGLE

Aquatics don't fail from lack of ambition. They fail from **trying to build everything, all at once, alone.**

They don't burn out like Deserts, or stall like Grasslands. They flood themselves with ideas, formats, possibilities, versions, worlds, and then they sink under the weight of their own brilliance.

They look around at the industry and see everything that's broken. And they're right, it *is* broken. But in trying to build an entirely new ecosystem, Aquatics often forget that you still need the old one to reach people.

You still need email. You still need a storefront. You still need a pitch. You still need *language* people already understand. You still need networks to amplify your message.

Aquatics want to burn down the system, but they also need to build bridges through it, at least long enough to get their audience across.

That's the contradiction that gets them stuck.

Aquatic pitfalls:

- **Overbuilding**: You try to create the whole vision at once—book, game, merch, lore, launch—and stall out from the sheer scope.
- **Undermarketing**: You can't explain the idea easily, so you either overexplain (walls of text) or go silent out of frustration.

- **Isolation**: You stop collaborating because no one "gets it" so you default to doing everything yourself.
- **Control obsession**: You can't delegate or partner because the vision is too specific and precious.
- **System rejection**: You refuse to use tools that are "too basic" or "too broken," but don't have viable alternatives in place.

And worst of all? You stop sharing *anything* because you believe the idea must be complete, perfect, and self-contained before the world is allowed to see it.

But if you wait until it's perfect? It dies in the dark.

WHAT AQUATICS NEED TO STAY HEALTHY

Aquatics don't need to scale back their ideas. They need to sequence them.

They don't need to give up control. They need to build systems that delegate wisely.

They don't need to sell out to the system. They need to use the system strategically while they build the new one.

Here's how Aquatics stay afloat and in motion.

1. BUILD THE WORLD IN PUBLIC

Perfection kills momentum. You don't need to finish everything before you share anything. You need:

- A public lore journal, blog, or podcast where you think out loud

- Behind-the-scenes development notes on Substack or Patreon
- A beta group who sees things *before* they're polished

Let your community witness the construction. That's how they learn to care.

2. PICK ONE ENTRY POINT AT A TIME

You can't onboard people into a ten-layer world. You need a front door. Just one.

- Choose one book, one platform, one format to lead with.
- Make that piece emotionally satisfying and narratively complete.
- Use it to *hook*, not explain.

The world can unfold later. The invitation comes first.

3. USE THE SYSTEM—DON'T LET IT USE YOU

Don't abandon email, newsletters, marketplaces, or social media just because they feel impersonal. Use them on *your terms*.

- Create an onboarding sequence that teaches people how to engage with your universe
- Use your website as a world map, not just a storefront
- Optimize one sales page, not ten

Treat every "basic" platform like an access point, not a compromise.

4. MAP THE VISION, STAGE THE DELIVERY

Your idea has 47 components. Good. You're not releasing all 47 at once.

- Create a 3–5 year roadmap for content and product releases
- Break your world into "phases" or "arcs," like a cinematic universe
- Use cross-format expansion *after* your core IP is stable

Aquatics don't need to shrink their dream. They need to release it in waves.

5. NAME THE TRANSLATORS

You need people who get it and can explain it better than you can.

- Recruit beta readers and ARC teams who can write the blurb *you can't*
- Partner with a Grassland to organize your world into usable language
- Find a Tundra to build a launch campaign that feels like a cultural moment

You're not trying to go viral. You're trying to build a shared reality, but others have to help you frame it.

BUILD YOUR AQUATIC STACK

Your stack isn't a marketing plan. It's a transport system to carry people into your universe, one layer at a time.

STEP 1: ESTABLISH THE CORE CANON

- Choose one product (book, game, story) to be your *lighthouse*
- This is what people share. This is what people pitch.
- Use every other format (lore, merch, wiki, podcast) to deepen that one core entry

STEP 2: CREATE A VISUALIZED MAP

- Build a simple infographic or landing page that shows the structure of your world
- Readers need to know where to go next. Don't make them guess.
- Link this map in your email, books, and socials

STEP 3: LAUNCH IN PHASES

- Don't blow everything in one go
- Plan for early access, stretch goals, collector's editions, and serial expansions
- Let each new release echo the last like ripples in deep water

STEP 4: ANCHOR THE ECOSYSTEM

- Set up your own store or central hub
- Use Kickstarter or direct sales to retain control
- Own your audience (email, Discord, membership platforms)

This world *is yours*. Don't give it away.

STEP 5: CULTIVATE YOUR TRANSLATORS

- Give early readers shared language and emotional hooks
- Run closed beta groups, ARC launches, and ambassador programs
- Ask them: *How would you explain this to a friend?*
- Use their words in your future messaging

You don't need to simplify your work. You need to share the translation responsibility.

STEP 6: EXPAND THROUGH TRUE COLLABORATION

Aquatics don't just make stories. They build worlds and worlds are meant to be inhabited.

You're not looking for assistants. You're looking for co-builders. People who write inside your universe, launch products with you, bring their own voice and audience into your world without breaking it.

This isn't about outsourcing. It's about scaling vision through shared authorship.

Collaboration for Aquatics looks like:

- **Co-authors or licensed creators** writing canon-adjacent stories in your world
- **Product partnerships**: artists, musicians, game designers, or merch collaborators co-launching lore-aligned products
- **Split-world events**: crossover anthologies, shared launches, or dual-run crowdfunding campaigns

- **Co-branded offers**: bundling your world's book with someone else's character deck, soundtrack, or themed tarot
- **Creator collectives** who build entire *ecosystems together,* each person owning a thread of the web

When done well, your collaborators don't dilute your brand. They expand its surface area. They help more people find their entry point. They make the weirdness more accessible. They carry part of the creative load *because they're building it with you.*

It needs to stay *coherent*. And nothing builds coherence faster than a small team building the same mythos from different angles.

Aquatics scale best when they stop asking, "How do I launch this alone?" And start asking, *"Who else is obsessed with this world and how do we build it together?"*

STEP 7: BUILD YOUR TEAM LIKE AN ECOSYSTEM

You're not building a project. You're building a creative enterprise, even if it still lives in your Dropbox folder.

At a certain point, Aquatics need more than collaborators. They need a team of people who are *dedicated to the ongoing growth and operation of the world you've built.*

Not just co-creators, but:

- **Project managers** to run timelines, launches, and contributor communication
- **Production partners** to format, print, ship, or manufacture

- **Operations leads** to managing budgeting, logistics, and fulfillment
- **Marketing coordinators** to write newsletters, manage swaps, and support visibility
- **Community managers** to run your Discord, collect testimonials, and activate superfans

In a healthy Aquatic stack, your job becomes:

- Vision holder
- Lore keeper
- Creative director
- Final gatekeeper

And the rest? Delegated. Intentionally. Repeatedly. Even if you can only afford 2–5 hours of help a week, start now. Build the muscle of handing things off. Learn how to write briefs, approve drafts, and *let go of the 20% that's keeping you underwater.*

BUILD THE WORLD, THEN BUILD THE BRIDGE

You're not here to play inside a broken system. You're here to replace it with something rich, strange, immersive, and true.

But the irony is that you still need the old system long enough to bring people into the new one.

So build the world, but also build the bridge. The translator. The pitch. The team. The entry point.

You can create something no one's ever seen, but no one will enter until you make it make sense.

That's not selling out. That's strategy.

Because once your world is visible? Once someone finally gets it?

They don't just follow. They *stay*. They *share*. They *expand it with you.*

Because nobody builds better than an Aquatic. They just have to remember that nobody who explores alone survives long.

CHAPTER 6

FINDING SUCCESS USING AUTHOR ECOSYSTEMS

One of the most common questions I get asked about The Author Ecosystems is, "Great. I know my ecosystem. What do I do now and why do I even care?"

The answer to that is as simple as it is complicated, but there is really only **one** reason why the Author Ecosystems exists; to help you find the quickest path to continuous, replicable, predictable success to create a stable, prosperous, sustainable career.

Getting to success quickly is the cornerstone of the Author Ecosystem strategy. That doesn't mean haphazard success, though. In the end, we only rise to the level of the structures we have in place. Yes, we might find success before we have the structures or language to support them, but it won't be lasting unless we build the mechanisms to find that success repeatedly.

The Author Ecosystems are meant to give you the language to contextualize your success and build the structures to support it.

If you're a ***Desert,*** for instance, you don't need to spend a lot of time building a mailing list. In fact, since you change your voice so often, it will probably be a drag on your success, because people will only stay with you until you change your voice again.

You might change your voice and genre every 3-6 months for years, and meanwhile you'll be pulling along people who don't resonate with anything you've written for a long time. Since you focus on virality and hijacking trends to help propel your message, you could have a very nice career without a mailing list at all.

Meanwhile, if you're a ***Forest,*** who mainly only writes one theme for their whole career and never focuses on trends, you would be silly not to put a ton of energy into your mailing list and community, but you probably don't have to ever look at social media to see what's trending because you will never, ever catch that trend (*except by luck*).

This whole archetyping system is meant to show you five different success paths you can use to go from zero to success quickly, how to build out the right foundations for that success, and then how to expand your business using the other ecosystems when you are ready to scale.

It all starts with finding ***one success path*** that delivers consistent, predictable, repeatable revenue. Finding one path to consistent revenue allows you to build a strong foundation for your career.

Everything we're doing in The Author Ecosystems is helping you find ***that one repeatable revenue stream*** that will keep delivering you results no matter what. Once we nail it down, you should be able to pull that lever every time you need a cash injection and have it deliver for you.

This focused approach reduces the complexity and drag that can come from juggling multiple strategies simultaneously. By channeling your efforts into a single, well-defined path, you can achieve critical mass more quickly, paving the way for future diversification and growth.

By progressing through these stages, creators can build a more stable and profitable business, reducing vulnerability to market changes and increasing their chances of long-term success.

For a *Grassland*, having at least a weekly blog and guesting on podcasts consistently are probably essential parts of their stack because they need to be seen as an authority in their niche, while a *Tundra* would only need to do that during a launch to help build excitement.

Everyone has a finite amount of energy, and if you're focusing on bits of other stacks that don't actually move the needle for you, then you are going to spin your wheels and burn yourself out. It's not that any of this stuff doesn't work. It just possibly doesn't work for you.

That's the whole point of our unofficial slogan "You're not doing marketing wrong. You're doing the wrong marketing.

Deserts probably need to spend all their time writing the next book and catching the next trend, so they don't have a lot of time for podcasts, mailing lists, social media, Facebook groups, etc. If they start doing those things, then they either won't have the energy for what matters, or they'll burn out trying to do everything. Their quickest path to success is writing the next book, while for an Aquatic, they need to be out in front of their brand acting like a ringleader, and probably hiring Deserts to work in their worlds to help fill it up with content.

For an **Aquatic**, they need to make everything an event that delighted superfans love, which takes all their energy, giving them very little back for their actual content, unless they hire well to build out the structures of their universe.

Do you see how important this is now? You shouldn't be doing 20% of all five ecosystems because then you won't get anywhere. All you'll do is burn out and negate all the work you're doing because you these actions are canceling each other out.

However, if you give 100% energy and keep doubling down on the actions that work, they keep compounding on themselves.

That is why your base ecosystem becomes the basis for your business. For me, as a Tundra, launching something on Kickstarter is the basis of my business. When I'm designing my year, those launches go in first and they are meant to deliver enough revenue that if I did nothing else they could keep me going.

My year looks a lot like a fashion designer. I have months where I rest, months where I launch, and months where I build. I'm a **Tundra**, and that process of Build, Launch, Recover is the essential rhythm to how I operate. Your ecosystem dictates the rhythm of your business and everything else radiates from it.

Even now that I've evolved into a more complex ecosystem, I still think about the Build, Launch, Recover cycle as an essential component of how I grow.

A *Desert's* rhythm involves hitting more singles than I do, and launching more often, but with a smaller spectacle than me with each launch (because they can't expend the same energy on each launch as I do since I've been resting for months). They probably release a book every month or two without a lot of fanfare, packaging those books into omnibuses every three books, and then packaging them all together every six books into a massive series omnibus. They are also likely using Vanessa Vale's Box Method and hiring a team to bring their work into other formats.

A *Grassland* is almost always in low-power mode, putting out content on a continuous, maybe even daily basis, guest blogging, guesting on podcasts, and caching amazing SEO for years as they build their dominance and help their niche become the next big thing. It looks like they are everywhere, but they are slowly putting pennies in the bank every day, while Tundras are tossing in hundred dollar bills every couple of months.

Tundras have the Build, Launch, Recover cycle. They are very seasonally ambitious who disappear when they aren't launching. We rest a lot because launches take a ton out of us. Our entire worlds tend to stop while we're in the launch part of our cycle.

Forests are mainly focused inside their communities, hyping up their diehard fans and providing them the language and ability to feel seen. They aren't out in the wide world much because they are giving everything to their community and turning them into ambassadors for their work. Then, when they launch, they rely on their communities to get the word out.

Aquatics are constantly finding new partnerships and delivering their universe into new formats. They are also planning events that get their fandom, and the broader world, excited about their work. Their partners do a lot of the heavy lifting during a launch with them in a support role much of the time, which means they can launch a whole lot more than anyone else, except maybe Deserts, since they are borrowing other people's audiences to do it.

Do you see how being half a **Grassland** and half a **Tundra** will burn you out? Their success paths are almost completely opposed to each other. Grasslands give a little bit all the time and Tundras give a ton in small bursts. I know because that's exactly what happened to Monica and I during our first year in business.

Writers, by and large, do not have any rhythm to their business, so they are always flailing and wondering how they'll make money. The Author Ecosystems is meant to give you the stability and focus to find the rhythm that you can dance to for the rest of your career.

Now that we have that out of the way, let's figure out the next steps.

DO YOU WANT TO EMBRACE THIS AUTHOR ECOSYSTEM?

The biggest misconception people have about The Author Ecosystems is that it is a personality test.

This is not Myers-Briggs. This is not Enneagrams. This is not even CliftonStrengths.

Instead, each one of us embodies all five ecosystems at all times to varying degrees. We can turn them on and off at will. So, **once you identify your dominant ecosystem, the first question is whether you want to embrace it.** You can wake up tomorrow and decide to transition from a Desert to a Forest if that aligns better with your goals and lifestyle.

Why would you do that? Maybe you don't like the rhythm of that business, or maybe you see that you can't sustain it. Maybe you are worn out and want to try something new, or maybe you got into a rhythm when you were first becoming an author, and it doesn't work for you anymore.

Heck, maybe you just think another ecosystem would be more fun. Either way, you aren't beholden to any ecosystem. However, whatever you choose, be prepared to go all in on it for the next 6-12 months because in order to break through the noise and get where you want to go, that's what it's probably going to take, following one path to success.

If you choose to change, congratulations! This marks the first day of a transformative journey.

EMBRACING YOUR ECOSYSTEM

Each ecosystem offers unique strengths and weaknesses. Understanding these can help you leverage your natural tendencies while addressing potential pitfalls.

DESERT ECOSYSTEM

Deserts excel in trend-spotting and quick production. They are adept at making unemotional business decisions, riding trends, and optimizing their processes. However, they need to balance short-term gains with long-term sustainability. The key for Deserts is to maintain a "camel hump" of resources to weather market changes and avoid overreliance on a single trend or niche.

Dan Brown and **E.L. James** are prime examples of successful Deserts. They capitalized on specific trends and delivered what readers wanted at the right time, achieving significant commercial success.

Desert Success Path

- **Harness Virality:** Watch social media and other outlets for signals on what is hot and harness it for your own success. Lots of romance authors are Deserts, and look at them all blowing up on TikTok.
- **Write the next book:** Don't get distracted by other tasks that aren't about harnessing virality and writing the next book.
- **Build a Publishing House:** Partner with other Deserts to create a stable of writers who can help you dominate a genre.

GRASSLAND ECOSYSTEM

Grasslands are deep delvers, focusing on popular topics that align with their interests. They become experts in their chosen fields and produce high-quality, best-in-class content. Grasslands need to avoid spreading themselves across too many projects and should focus on building a strong foundation in one area before expanding.

George R.R. Martin exemplifies the Grassland ecosystem. His deep and detailed world-building in the "A Song of Ice and Fire" series has created a dedicated fan base and lasting legacy.

Grassland Success Path

- **Leverage Content Marketing:** Expand your reach by creating a blog, podcast, or YouTube channel centered around your niche.
- **Collaborate with Experts:** Partner with thought leaders in adjacent fields to enhance your authority and reach.
- **Expand Your Series:** Develop long series, spin-offs, sequels, or companion books to deepen your audience's engagement.

TUNDRA ECOSYSTEM

Tundras are natural launchers and trend stackers. They excel at creating excitement and maximizing the impact of their launches. However, they need to manage their feast-and-famine cycles effectively and ensure they have enough resources to sustain them between launches.

Tim Ferriss and **Sherrilyn Kenyon** are notable Tundras. They have mastered the art of launching projects that capture significant attention and generate substantial revenue.

Tundra Success Path

- **Stack Evergreen Trends:** Incorporate multiple evergreen trends into your launches to maximize their impact.
- **Optimize Your Launch Process:** Refine your launch strategies based on past successes and failures.
- **Explore New Platforms:** Experiment with platforms like Kickstarter or Patreon to diversify your income.

FOREST ECOSYSTEM

Forests thrive on interconnectivity and personal touch. They often juggle multiple pen names and genres, injecting their personality into all their works. The strength of a Forest lies in the shared language and consistent nurturing of their projects. However, they must avoid spreading themselves too thin and focus on leveraging their personal brand to build a loyal audience.

For example, **Stephen King** and **Brandon Sanderson** have successfully created vast interconnected worlds that captivate their readers. Their ability to maintain consistency across different genres while staying true to their unique voice is a hallmark of the Forest ecosystem.

Forest Success Path

- **Cross-Pollinate Your Projects:** Use your different pen names and genres to create interconnected worlds and series.
- **Develop a Strong Personal Brand:** Focus on building a close relationship with your readers through personalized engagement.
- **Leverage Fan Engagement:** Utilize platforms like Ream or Patreon to foster a strong community around your work.

AQUATIC ECOSYSTEM

Aquatics are versatile creators who thrive on building immersive experiences for their audience. They often work across multiple formats and platforms, tailoring their strategies to their fans' preferences. The challenge for Aquatics is to avoid spreading themselves too thin and to maintain a coherent brand across different formats.

Michael Crichton is a successful Aquatic, known for his expansive worlds and ability to engage readers across various media, including books, audiobooks, and graphic novels.

Aquatic Success Path

- **Expand into Multiple Formats:** Offer your stories in various formats, such as graphic novels, audiobooks, and web series.
- **Develop Immersive Experiences:** Create a rich multimedia experience for your audience, including merchandise and fan events.

- **Build a Strong Team:** Delegate tasks to a team that shares your vision to expand your creative output.

Understanding your Author Ecosystem is just the beginning. By asking the right questions and strategically maximizing and evolving your ecosystem, you can achieve sustainable success in your author career. Embrace your natural tendencies, focus on your strengths, and methodically expand your strategies to reach new heights.

Start doubling down on the strengths of your ecosystem today, shed what's not working, and pave the way to your ultimate success.

The journey to mastering your Author Ecosystem is ongoing. Embrace change, stay committed to your goals, and remember that success is about finding and optimizing the right path for you. Whether you're a Desert, Grassland, Tundra, Forest, or Aquatic, there's a clear path to thriving in the ever-evolving world of authorship.

CHAPTER 7

THE EVOLUTION PATH OF EACH AUTHOR ECOSYSTEM

We've talked a lot about ecosystems already, but knowing your ecosystem is only half of the Author Ecosystems equation. The other half is knowing your evolution path.

Monica Leonelle and I did a lot of research this past year, both digging into data and having conversations with writers about their businesses. We found there are five evolution levels in a writer's career. Knowing both your ecosystem and your evolution level allows you to triangulate the advice you take and the advice you give to others.

Here are the five levels we found through our research. Please remember, these ecosystems are about marketing and sales success, so *if you are not even ready to think about that kind of thing, then you would be a Level 0.*

- **Level 1 -** *Inert.* Authors at this level don't even know how to start doing things because it's so overwhelming. They are pulled in every direction and feel like they are drowning in information from every direction. In order to get out of this level, you need to start doing something and it doesn't matter much what you do.
- **Level 2 -** *Developing.* Authors at this level have started doing things, which is great, but nothing is working. They are following all the best practices as best they

can, but they are failing at everything they try. If you want to get to the next level, you have to find something that works and latch onto it. ***NOTE:*** *You probably won't know your ecosystem until you get out of this stage, and that's okay. Until you know what works, you are just using what feels right to you. Once you know what works, then you'll have a better handle on it.*

- **Level 3 - *Emergent.*** Authors at this level have found something that works, but they are also doing all sorts of other things that aren't working. To get out of this level, you need to shed everything that's not working and double down on things that are working for your ecosystem.
- **Level 4 - *Evolved.*** Authors at this level have fully embraced their ecosystem and are making money, but they are capped out at what they can earn without evolving beyond what they've been doing. In order to exit this level, you need to integrate other ecosystems into your author business.
- **Level 5 - *Expanded.*** At this top level, authors have found ways to integrate new bits into their business that help them continuously grow.

If you know you are a level 3 Desert (we call that a ***D3***), then so much suddenly becomes clear to you. For instance, you know that the thing you should be focused on right now is optimizations to get from level 3 to level 4. You also know you should be focusing on finding the next hottest trope in your genre and writing a bunch of books in it before the arbitrage goes away.

You also know that you should be focused on learning from other Deserts who can help you embrace the qualities that will help you thrive. Conversely, if you're a level 4 Desert (***D4***), then you know that you should be focused on learning from other ecosystems to help you expand.

One of the biggest things that hampers authors is that they try to expand too quickly into other ecosystems. While you should be testing things to find what works at level 2, once you have found those things that work you should be shedding everything else in level 3 to double down on what's working to push through into success. Once you have had success, ***then and only then*** should you start adding other ecosystems back into your business.

Each stage has its own growth metrics.

- **Are you inert?** Then you need to settle and start somewhere, anywhere.
- **Are you developing?** Keep testing and experimenting with different ecosystems to find something that works for you.
- **Are you emergent?** It's time to double down on what's working and cut things that aren't so you can focus your attention and find success.
- **Are you evolved?** Now it's time to start integrating new things into your business to allow you to build.
- **Are you expanding?** Awesome. Keep going.

One thing to remember about these levels is that you can ascend or descend them. Authors often think that once they are a level 3, they can never descend back to level 2, but more often than not this descent is a major cause of burnout.

Strategies that have worked for years can suddenly start failing, which causes an author to double down and double down again, losing ground with each iteration until they collapse in a heap from exhaustion.

This is why it's so important to double down quickly once you find something that works, so you can create a stable income and then start incorporating other ecosystems into your business before those strategies lose efficacy.

Most authors become stuck in level 3, getting distracted by shiny objects while their business stagnates and they fall back into level 2, only to continue that cycle again and again until they burn out. If instead we can double down on what's working quickly without getting distracted, then we can push through level 3 and start building out systems in level 4 to make our businesses more resilient.

The vast majority of authors we talk to are stuck between level 2 and level 3. They are either floundering to find something that works or using all their energy on actions that don't work instead of focusing on those things that do.

Most authors will never get out of level 3 because they are bogged down with actions that have marginal efficacy to them. Instead, they are in a continuous cycle between level 2 and level 3. They are so tired that they can't get enough momentum to achieve escape velocity into level 4.

But, let's say you have reached level 4, **how do you evolve beyond your ecosystem?** After all, focusing on one ecosystem for a while is great, and gives you something to fall back on in times of trouble, but a robust author business needs multiple ecosystems and streams of income working together so that when one fails they can pivot their business quickly.

We've charted evolution paths for each ecosystem, and while there are commonalities between them, each one is unique.

As we go through this, it's important to remember that when we talk about "evolving into an ecosystem", we aren't telling you to abandon your base ecosystem. Instead, you are incorporating aspects of the other ecosystems into your business in ways that make sense to create a stronger author business.

I've outlined possible evolution paths for each ecosystem, though you might see something different in your business that makes you take a different path.

DESERT

- **Forest** - Forests are the most antithetical to Deserts, but creating a shared language and making your books stickier solves one of the biggest Desert weaknesses, creating ephemeral books that stop generating revenue quickly. Forests are great at creating a shared language, and we think you should be incorporating that part earlier in your journey.
- **Aquatic** - Most Deserts want to evolve into Aquatics first, but Aquatics are the hardest and most expensive to get going, and the most superfan focused. That said, you know how to drive traffic, and now that you've gotten your books hookier, you can start turning all those casual readers into superfans.

- **Grassland** - Since both Deserts and Grasslands are data-heavy ecosystems, it's relatively easy for Deserts to start incorporating longer series and content marketing into their businesses.
- **Tundra** - Since Deserts are TOFU experts and Tundras are BOFU experts, you'll supercharge your ecosystem by being able to create irresistible offers that your newly minted superfans will love.

GRASSLAND

- **Tundra** - Grasslands are all flywheel, and Tundras are all funnel, so it makes sense to start your evolution journey by embracing your inner Tundra. The biggest problem for a Grassland is standing up and saying, "Did you know you could buy this?" That is the biggest strength of a Tundra.
- **Forest** - Forests are all about shared language and developing a community of readers who can communicate with each other, which would be a huge asset for a Grassland, who generally have the ear of influential people and can move the direction of an industry already because of their intense grasp of their topic, but don't have a shared language to bring people deeper into their universe.
- **Aquatic** - Aquatics focus heavily on slow growth and super-fandom. They are building their own category across many years, which aligns with Grassland's desire to be future-focused. However, Grasslands are moving the industry to a point on the horizon that is inevitable, so that when the industry arrives there they are the authority. Meanwhile, Aquatics are shining a light on something that nobody even knows they need,

which is almost antithetical to the ethos of the Grassland. For that reason, it probably makes sense to leave Aquatic evolution toward the end of your journey.

- **Desert** - Grasslands are very long-term focused, while Deserts are concerned with immediate success. While we don't think Grasslands should immediately start embracing the short-term wins that come easily to a Desert, being able to capture attention by using existing virality can help funnel readers into the largesse of a Grassland's catalog.

TUNDRA

- **Aquatic** - Aquatics take the longest to spin up for most ecosystems, but Tundras are great at injecting cash infusions into a business, so it would make sense to start this work from the beginning of your evolution journey. You should also be thinking about creating your category across every launch from the beginning of your career. It will just take a long time to bring everything together, but for a Tundra, you should be thinking about your category from your first launch, and how to make each one feed into an overall whole. The more you can use your launches to complement each other, the better you'll be in the long run.
- **Grassland** - A Tundra is a funnel without a flywheel, and a Grassland is a great flywheel, especially when it comes to attracting new people into their orbit. Tundras desperately need somewhere to send people who get through their funnel and to warm new people up so they're excited for their next project. Whether it's a Grassland or an Aquatic, Tundras grow best when they have one huge universe or topic to pour all their work

into so it keeps growing over time. Even if you're writing a lot of disparate things, think about putting them under one umbrella so that all your effort isn't wasted after each launch.

- **Desert** - Deserts are masters of the opt-in while Tundras are the masters of the irresistible offer. Once you have your ecosystem solid, then it's time to keep funneling people in and learning how to do it on autopilot.
- **Forest** - Creating a shared language between your launches will help you craft a narrative to bring your disparate projects together in an umbrella everyone can use to get excited about your work.

FOREST

- **Grassland** - You have a pretty great retention and escalation path for people to fall in love with. However, you'll get a lot out of taking your shared language and creating longer series with better content marketing around them. Studying data like a Grassland will help you make better long-term decisions once you have some stability under you.
- **Desert** - Since you already have great engagement, now it's time to bring people into your universe. Combined with your inner Grassland, a Desert will constantly bring in leads and readers into your orbit.
- **Tundra** - Forests take a long time to grow, but they grow quicker if they can create big spectacle launches that help bring attention to their work, and the more you can use evergreen tropes to help draw attention to your work. Both of these are huge strengths of a Tundra.

- **Aquatic** - Forests are great at engaging with fans, and Aquatics are the ultimate superfan ecosystem. They are all about delighting their fans, and creating a huge epic universe across many formats for them to play in once they join up. While your ecosystem grows slowly, you can be using Aquatic tactics to help monetize them across many different mediums.

AQUATIC

- **Desert** - Getting better at opt-ins is something that will bring a lot more people into your universe. You already know how to turn casual readers into superfans, so let's start by driving people into your ecosystem en masse.
- **Tundra** - It's really expensive to be an Aquatic, and Tundras are great at bringing cash infusions into their businesses. You need that since your plans are generally so epic in scope and span many modalities.
- **Forest** - Once you have money coming into your business, you need a better way to engage with your readers by creating a shared language between them and facilitating ways for them to talk to each other. This is the strength of a Forest, and embracing that evolution can broaden the appeal of your work.
- **Grassland** - Grasslands are all about depth, and a big, massive universe needs a ton of depth. Whether it's world bibles, shared universes, RPGs, or any number of formats, embracing your inner Grassland will help give your world depth that will delight readers and bring them deeper into your universe.

As you can see, the evolution paths for each ecosystem can be wildly different. There's a reason why we didn't number these paths. There's a lot of fluidity between them as well, which might make you evolve two paths at once.

I hope you can also see how important it is not to start rushing into these evolutions before your base ecosystem is working well for you. It's a lot of new concepts and modalities to add to your workflow when you haven't had sustained success yet. You will likely collapse under the weight of it if you don't have a solid stream of income in place first.

When I say you should be stripping those things that don't work and double down on what's working, that doesn't mean forever. It means until you have consistent revenue coming in and have breathing room to start looking at the biggest picture.

Until you get there, you'll be scrambling just to survive. Evolution comes when you have that space to grow beyond what you are doing, and that comes with time.

Even once you're ready to evolve, you shouldn't try to incorporate more than one ecosystem a quarter into your business, and maybe even one a year. Evolution is about the long-term stability of your business, which only comes after getting short-term stability in your business.

CHAPTER 8

BLENDED ECOSYSTEMS FOR WRITERS

In nature, ecosystems often blend at their edges, creating rich environments where two biomes coexist. For authors, these blended ecosystems represent a mix of creative tendencies and strategies that combine the strengths of two archetypes. However, blending ecosystems also brings challenges. Writers must learn to harness both sides without becoming overwhelmed by competing tendencies. Below, we'll explore six common blended ecosystems in detail and how writers can thrive in each.

SAVANNAH: THE FOCUSED TREND RIDER (DESERT/GRASSLAND)

The **Savannah** ecosystem is a writer's blend of quick trend adaptation and deep-rooted focus. Writers in this ecosystem are great at identifying emerging opportunities like a **Desert** while also grounding themselves in the thought leadership and long-term planning of a **Grassland**. They chase relevant trends, quickly producing content that hits the market at the right time, but they also have the discipline to build a strong, long-term brand.

Strengths:

- **Quick responsiveness to trends**: Savannah writers are excellent at spotting emerging trends and acting on them swiftly, giving them an edge in content that feels fresh, relevant, and timely.

- **Grounded in a core niche**: Unlike writers who spread themselves too thin by chasing every trend, Savannah writers maintain a strong focus on a central topic or niche (Grassland), which gives them credibility and expertise.

- **Balance of speed and substance**: This combination allows writers to gain visibility in the short-term through trending topics, while ensuring their content has lasting value due to its depth.

Challenges:

- **Risk of trend-chasing without depth**: The Desert's tendency to jump on trends quickly might make it difficult to maintain depth. Writers in the Savannah ecosystem must guard against sacrificing quality for speed.

- **Burnout from trying to stay relevant**: Constantly monitoring trends while also nurturing a long-term niche can be exhausting. If not managed properly, the drive to stay on top of everything could lead to creative fatigue.

- **Perception of being a trend-hopper**: There's a risk that audiences might see Savannah writers as overly opportunistic if they're not careful to balance trend-driven content with genuine expertise.

Actionable Steps:

- **Set clear boundaries for trend adoption**: Don't chase every trend. Focus on those that align with your long-term goals and complement your niche expertise.

- **Create evergreen content**: While staying on top of trends is important, balance it with content that remains valuable even after the trend fades.

- **Use timeboxing**: Allocate specific periods to focus on trend-driven content and others to focus on deep, evergreen material, ensuring you don't get burned out or distracted by too many short-term goals.

BRAMBLE: THE DEEP DIVER WITH PERSONAL FLAIR (GRASSLAND/FOREST)

The **Bramble** ecosystem blends the focused, grounded work of **Grassland** writers with the personal, emotional engagement of **Forest** creators. Writers here are experts in their field, delivering high-quality content on a specific niche while also sharing their personality and personal experiences. The result is deep, thoughtful content infused with relatable, human touches that resonate strongly with readers.

Strengths:

- **Master of a niche with personal engagement**: Bramble writers are not only experts in their field, but they also bring a personal voice that makes their content feel relatable and engaging. Their depth of knowledge (Grassland) combined with personal storytelling (Forest) fosters loyalty among readers.

- **Stronger reader connections**: The Forest aspect allows Bramble writers to build an emotional bond with their audience. Readers don't just come for the information—they return for the author's unique perspective and personality.

- **Authenticity**: Writers in the Bramble ecosystem often come across as more genuine because their work blends expertise with personal insight, making their content feel more like a conversation than a lecture.

Challenges:

- **Struggle to maintain consistency**: Balancing the desire to share personal stories and maintaining authority in a niche can be difficult. Writers might veer too far into personal territory, losing their focus on delivering valuable information.

- **Vulnerability fatigue**: Constantly drawing from personal experience can be emotionally draining. Forest writers often put their heart and soul into their work, which can lead to burnout if they don't set boundaries.

- **Niche vs. breadth tension**: Bramble writers may feel torn between staying focused on their niche (Grassland) and expanding into more personal, diverse topics (Forest), which can create internal conflict over their content strategy.

Actionable Steps:

- **Set content boundaries**: Be clear on where personal stories add value and where they distract.

Use personal anecdotes to enhance, not overshadow, your expertise.

- **Establish a personal-niche ratio**: Aim to have a balance in your content that blends 80% expertise and 20% personal narrative, or another ratio that suits your goals and audience.

- **Plan breaks**: Personal writing can be exhausting. Schedule regular time off to avoid vulnerability fatigue and protect your emotional energy.

GLACIER: THE LAUNCH EXPERT WITH STAYING POWER (TUNDRA/GRASSLAND)

Glacier writers embody the high-energy, exciting launches of the **Tundra**, combined with the **Grassland**'s steady, long-term content production. These writers know how to create buzz around new projects, and they have the discipline to sustain that momentum over time with focused, detailed work. While some writers excel at either the excitement of launches or the grind of long-term content, Glacier writers master both.

Strengths:

- **Great at building anticipation**: Glacier writers excel at using high-energy, launch-focused strategies to generate excitement and build an initial audience.

- **Long-term commitment**: Once the launch excitement fades, they're able to maintain and grow their audience with sustained, in-depth work, giving them an edge over writers who fade post-launch.

- **Master of launch cycles**: Glacier writers understand how to create momentum, using launches as strategic touchpoints throughout the year, and capitalizing on the energy of each one to further deepen their content.

Challenges:

- **Difficulty maintaining the energy**: Tundra energy is intense, and Glacier writers may struggle to keep up that level of excitement throughout the year, especially if they are also trying to nurture long-term projects.

- **Launch burnout**: Constantly creating and managing launches can be overwhelming. Writers in this ecosystem must be careful to pace themselves or risk burning out from the pressure of frequent promotional cycles.

- **Balancing excitement with content depth**: The focus on high-energy launches can sometimes overshadow the need for depth, especially if the writer feels pressured to move on quickly to the next project without fully developing the current one.

Actionable Steps:

- **Strategically space out launches**: Don't feel pressured to launch too often. Space out high-energy moments to allow for downtime and deeper work in between.

- **Use momentum wisely**: Capitalize on the energy of a launch to build deeper, more evergreen content that your audience can return to after the buzz dies down.

- **Plan post-launch recovery time**: Always schedule time to rest after a major launch. This will help you avoid burnout and allow you to refocus on the more in-depth aspects of your work.

TIAGA: THE PASSIONATE BUILDER WITH A PERSONAL TOUCH (TUNDRA/FOREST)

The **Tiaga** ecosystem blends the **Tundra**'s love of high-energy launches with the **Forest**'s nurturing, personal engagement. Writers in this ecosystem build strong initial excitement for their work but also focus on fostering long-term, personal connections with their audience. Tiaga writers excel at blending big, bold ideas with heartfelt, emotionally-driven content, ensuring that their readers stay invested long after the launch buzz fades.

Strengths:

- **Incredible audience engagement**: Tiaga writers are great at making their audience feel like part of the journey, building deep, emotional connections through personal stories and engagement.

- **High visibility with authenticity**: The combination of energetic launches and personal content creates a winning formula—readers are drawn to the excitement but stay for the authentic connection.

- **Fan loyalty**: Because Tiaga writers engage deeply with their audience on a personal level, their readers often become loyal fans, eager to support their future work.

Challenges:

- **Difficulty balancing launch energy and personal connections**: The high-energy demands of launching new projects can make it difficult to maintain the personal, nurturing relationships required to keep readers engaged.

- **Risk of emotional exhaustion**: Constantly pouring personal stories and energy into your audience can lead to burnout, especially if you're also managing the intensity of Tundra-style launches.

- **Over-reliance on personal engagement**: While personal stories build loyalty, they may distract from delivering consistent, high-quality content. Tiaga writers must balance their personal touch with strong, valuable content.

Actionable Steps:

- **Automate audience engagement where possible**: Use tools to manage your community and handle routine interactions, giving you more time to focus on content creation and personal touchpoints that matter.

- **Build in downtime after launches**: Tiaga writers should schedule dedicated rest periods after major launches to recharge emotionally and creatively.

- **Create content that speaks for itself**: Make sure that your content is strong enough to stand on its own, without relying entirely on personal connections to keep your audience engaged.

ARCTIC: THE IMMERSIVE EXPERIENCE CREATOR (TUNDRA/AQUATIC)

The **Arctic** ecosystem is where the **Tundra**'s fast-paced launch strategies meet the **Aquatic** ecosystem's expansive, immersive content experience. Arctic writers are great at pulling their audience into a rich, multi-faceted world that spans various formats, from books to podcasts to merchandise. Their work is both fast-paced and deeply immersive, keeping readers engaged with a world they can explore long after the initial launch excitement fades.

Strengths:

- **Master of multi-platform content**: Arctic writers know how to create immersive experiences that pull readers in through multiple formats, giving them a wide reach and deep engagement.

- **Ability to generate buzz and sustain it**: They can capitalize on the Tundra's launch energy to build excitement, but they keep the momentum going by offering more than just one format of content, keeping readers engaged long-term.

- **Cross-platform loyalty**: Their audience often follows them across different media, creating a strong, loyal fanbase that engages with their work on multiple levels (e.g., reading, listening, and buying).

Challenges:

- **Managing complexity**: The Arctic ecosystem involves juggling multiple formats (audio, visual, written), which can be overwhelming for a writer who is also trying to launch and promote.

- **Content overload**: With so many moving parts, Arctic writers risk creating an overwhelming amount of content that's hard for their audience to keep up with, or that dilutes the overall brand.

- **Time management**: The fast pace of Tundra launches combined with the deep immersion of Aquatic ecosystems can lead to burnout if the writer doesn't carefully manage their time.

Actionable Steps:

- **Use delegation or automation**: Consider hiring a team or using automation tools to handle some of the multi-platform logistics, allowing you to focus on creativity and content.

- **Plan staggered content**: Release different formats of content in phases to avoid overwhelming your audience and give yourself time to focus on quality over quantity.

- **Leverage cross-promotion**: Use the buzz from each new launch to drive attention to your other formats, ensuring that each piece of content builds off the last.

SWAMP: THE MULTI-PASSIONATE CONNECTOR (FOREST/AQUATIC)

In the **Swamp** ecosystem, writers combine the **Forest**'s deep, personal engagement with the **Aquatic**'s multi-format, immersive experience. These writers excel at making their audience feel emotionally connected to their work, while offering a wide range of content across various platforms, whether it's through writing, podcasts, merchandise, or events. The Swamp ecosystem allows for rich creative exploration across multiple avenues, providing a deeply interconnected experience for readers.

Strengths:

- **Strong personal connections**: Swamp writers excel at building close-knit communities, making their audience feel personally invested in their work and career.

- **Diverse content ecosystem**: They are able to provide a range of content across different formats, allowing for multiple entry points to engage with their audience.

- **Holistic brand experience**: Swamp writers often build a cohesive, well-rounded brand that resonates with fans, making them more likely to support the writer across various platforms and media.

Challenges:

- **Overextension**: Managing multiple formats while maintaining deep emotional connections can spread

Swamp writers too thin, potentially leading to burnout or loss of quality.

- **Difficulty maintaining focus**: With so many creative projects happening across various platforms, it can be easy to lose focus or let certain elements fall by the wayside, leading to inconsistencies in content or brand messaging.

- **Audience segmentation**: When offering so many different formats, there's a risk of fragmenting your audience—some may prefer podcasts, others written work, making it harder to keep a unified fanbase.

Actionable Steps:

- **Set clear priorities**: Focus on one or two main platforms at a time, ensuring each format gets the attention it deserves before expanding to other areas.

- **Cross-pollinate content**: Ensure that each piece of content across formats ties into your overall brand and message, making it easier for your audience to follow you between platforms.

- **Create community hubs**: Use platforms like social media groups or newsletters to bring your audience together in one place, helping them feel connected to you and each other, regardless of which format they engage with.

Blended ecosystems offer unique opportunities for authors to harness the best of two worlds, but they also present challenges. Balancing these ecosystems takes careful planning and self-awareness, but when done right, it allows writers to reach new heights both creatively and financially.

Whether you're combining the trend-savvy nature of the **Savannah** with the deep focus of the **Bramble**, or mixing the high-energy **Glacier** with the immersive **Arctic**, finding your unique blend can help you build a sustainable and rewarding writing career.

As you go through the rest of this book, think about how to take the best from each part of your blended ecosystem to build a strong foundation for success.

CHAPTER 9

HOW I "EVOLVED" BEYOND MY NATURAL AUTHOR ECOSYSTEM

At this point, it's probably not hard to recognize that I'm a natural Tundra. I'm a seasonal launcher who took to Kickstarter like a fish to water or a polar bear to hibernation. I'm a world-class hype man who knows how to build excitement around a launch, which has served me well for the last decade.

However, over time I started to cap out on what I could do inside my natural ecosystem. This happens to most authors who have a healthy ecosystem. They find a natural limit to how much growth they can have doing the same thing over and over again.

I could predict a launch down to the dollar, but I didn't grow substantially between 2017-2020. I was still a six-figure creative during all those years, but just barely.

On top of that, the landscape was constantly changing under me, and it became harder and harder to get people excited about every new project I had coming out. Even though I didn't know the word back then, it was time for my ecosystem to evolve beyond just my Tundra instincts.

Evolving is the process of taking a healthy ecosystem and adding elements of the other ecosystems to help fuel growth. It should **only** be attempted once you have a stable ecosystem that is rocking and rolling predictably. *One of the biggest causes of authors having an unhealthy ecosystem is that they try to evolve too soon.*

I'm going to say it again because I know writers are stubborn. *Evolution should only be attempted once your ecosystem is healthy and stable*. Your ecosystem absolutely must be able to run predictably without much variation because you need that stable income to fuel your growth, and you need the brain space available to start taking on new tasks that are outside of your comfort zone.

Almost all authors that fail at doing this end up evolving too quickly and destroying their ecosystem. This happened to me, as well, and I had to spend years rebuilding my processes after they collapsed. It wasn't until my ecosystem was stable and predictable that these strategies started to work for me.

If you evolve too quickly, your existing ecosystem will devolve quickly, and you'll have to abandon your growth plans in order to nurse it back to health, wasting time and effort. Instead, *first focus on stabilizing and nurturing your own ecosystem so that it can operate nearly independently from you.*

Even though I know for a fact that many people reading this, even with my warnings, will think it's a good idea to evolve before they are ready, three warnings are all I have time for today. So, I'm going to move on and explain the strategies I used to build out my business beyond my ecosystem.

HOW I STABILIZED MY OWN ECOSYSTEM SO I COULD EVOLVE LIKE A TUNDRA

Like many authors, I tried to evolve beyond my ecosystem before it was stable and success kept slipping out from under me. Whether it was writing to market, rapid releasing, expanding beyond books into other formats, building interconnected books, forming communities, or trying to "own a topic", none of them worked because every time I stepped out of the thing I was good at, everything I had built would crumble under me.

Now I know the reason I failed is because I kept trying to move beyond my natural ecosystem before it was stable and predictable, but back then I just thought I was a failure.

Over time I learned all about the benefit of launching in seasons from JA Huss and Marc Jacobs, with quick bursts of live launching followed by long periods of recovery. ***This is the natural happy place for a Tundra.***

I created a system where I would launch four main campaigns a year, with time to recover and rebuild my email list between them. Since I couldn't hype up Kickstarters for a full month each campaign, I also started to cycle my campaigns at varying lengths from 5 days all the way up to 45 days depending on the marketing demands and budgets of each campaign.

I eventually settled on doing a novel launch in January, a graphic novel/anthology launch in March, another novel series launch in June, and a comic book launch in

September, with an experimental mini-launch in November for a small fandom-specific project.

Varying up my campaigns and keeping to that schedule stabilized my income and allowed me to start thinking about expanding. It took a couple of years to stabilize, but by 2022 I was ready to expand out from my Tundra roots and evolve into something new. Below is the order in which I evolved that worked for me, though every ecosystem has its own evolution path.

HOW I STARTED TO THINK LIKE A BRAND MANAGER AND EVOLVE LIKE AN AQUATIC

The biggest strength of an Aquatic ecosystem lies in their ability to develop systems to expand across different formats and involve different partners to grow their entire ecosystem. Unhealthy Aquatics expand too quickly before the scaffolding is in place, but a healthy Aquatic understands how to build out their brand without collapsing under the weight of it.

This idea is naturally appealing to most ecosystems because they can rely on other people to help them build their brand. Unfortunately, for other ecosystems, the books drive everything else, including growth. For Aquatics, their growth is fueled by their entire brand, so they should be branching out into other formats well before everyone else.

Meanwhile, Tundras like me need to point back to successful books in order to be taken seriously by brand partners. I tried to put together brand deals for years, but it wasn't until I started to focus on launching books continuously that those successful launches started to bear fruit.

In the end, I didn't need to do much beyond showing my books were popular to open dialog with board game companies, coffee brands, and RPGs. Often, they came to me, once I showed my brand had a critical mass of interest on a platform.

The growth of the game and publishing categories on Kickstarter certainly helped other companies take an interest in my brand, but only because I dug in deep on making my books popular on Kickstarter first, drumming up excitement, and using that to catapult my business into its evolution.

The key to my expansion was rooted directly in my Tundra ecosystem. The key to evolution isn't abandoning your ecosystem for another one, it's in using your natural state to fuel your expansion.

For me, the first successful expansion of my brand came from Monica incorporating my work into her Book Sales Supercharged series, specifically through the launch of *Get Your Book Selling on Kickstarter*.

Before I licensed my work to Monica, all the deals I was part of fell apart. Working with her was my first foray into expanding my brand beyond my own company that worked.

HOW I STARTED TO GO DEEPER WITH MY WORK AND EVOLVE LIKE A GRASSLAND

I started my career launching stand-alone books like the first volume of Ichabod Jones: Monster Hunter, Katrina Hates the Dead, and My Father Didn't Kill Himself.

Building excitement for a single book is one of the great skills of Tundras, and for the first years of my career, it worked really well. However, it eventually became apparent that the lack of depth in my catalog meant there was nothing to keep people coming back to read more about the universes they loved, which stifled my growth as an author.

It turns out, while people do read cross-genre more than anyone gives them credit for, they didn't do it enough to make a decent profit on a short fantasy series. For genres outside of romance and thriller, it generally takes four to five books before you can reasonably expect to make a profit on ads, which meant I had to write more books in the same series in order to fuel growth.

Since I didn't want to write in either of those genres, I decided that I needed to write a 10+ book signature series that could keep finding new fans for the rest of my career.

There is no doubt that this is a Grassland strategy as they are all about going deep on a few topics. However, I used my ability to gather excitement to launch not one but three signature series on Kickstarter (Ichabod Jones: Monster Hunter, The Godsverse Chronicles, and The Obsidian Spindle Saga). Instead of launching each book individually,

I chose to launch multiple books with each campaign to garner more attention from my audience and direct the narrative.

While you can find Ichabod Jones: Monster Hunter on retailers, neither The Godsverse Chronicles nor The Obsidian Spindle Saga have even launched on retailers and yet I've already earned back all the money I spent on creating them and built a nest egg for marketing. When they do launch, I can use my skills as a Tundra to build excitement again to help that launch succeed far into the future.

HOW I STARTED TO INTERCONNECT ALL MY WORK AND EVOLVE LIKE A FOREST

As a Tundra, I've developed a whole lot more successful stand-alone books than most other ecosystems, but in order to have long-term reader growth, I needed to connect them all together like a Forest.

In order to do this, I first needed to find my "shade trees". These were the books/series that stood out above all the others and attracted readers into my ecosystem and made them fall in love with my work.

Luckily, because of my work building out three deep series like a Grassland, I had three different shade trees to attract readers. However, they were all pointing to different universes without much interplay between them. In order to get readers excited to read my whole back catalog, I needed to find a way to connect them together.

I found that interconnectivity by creating The Cosmic Weave, a unifying concept I built around my books to connect my three biggest series together with my standalone work in an effort to increase reader retention.

I've created the mechanics for nearly all my books to connect together into one singular, satisfying experience for readers. It will take one more book to fully explain the concept, but once that capstone book launches, I'll have nearly everything interconnected for the rest of my career, building the bonds of my series like a Forest.

This interconnectivity is my attempt to evolve like a Forest, but it is fueled by my ability to build excitement and launch like a Tundra. Being able to launch a book successfully and break even on it allowed time for a lush Forest to grow with dozens of entry points that can drive audience growth for years.

HOW I STARTED TO FOLLOW THE TRENDS AND EVOLVE LIKE A DESERT

Of all the ecosystems, the one I struggle with the most is thinking like a Desert. Their superpower is finding attention arbitrage where demand far outstrips supply and delivering experiences readers gobble up with gusto.

This ability defined the career of pulp writers for generations, but I struggle with it. I have a deep-seated desire to embed my personality into everything I do and focus solely on the things that catch my interest even if nobody else cares about it.

For Deserts, knowing the hot tropes and delivering a satisfying experience audiences respond to is the goal, even if it means being invisible to the reader. Deserts make great ghostwriters, journalists, and licensed content writers because they can separate themselves from the work and be proud of whatever they are paid to write, even if they have no interest in it. They get excited to write a book optimized to hit as many hot trends, or client requirements, as possible, even if it means their voice is muted. Getting the story to pop with readers is the most important thing to Deserts, not infusing themselves into every page.

I envy that ability. I have no patience for or interest in optimization. I got in my own way when it came to money countless times for innumerable reasons. I've eschewed big genres with massive paydays because my artistic muse flitted to some obscure topic or another. I've turned away from life-changing offers because I didn't care much about the work. I even blew up successful companies just because I didn't feel like doing it anymore, even if it meant disappointing lots of people.

My friend told me once "what does it matter if you like it as long as people want to pay you for it", and I scoffed at them while my bank account withered.

It literally took 40 years of my life for me to understand that, when money comes easily, the rest of your life gets easier. So, I'm trying really hard to embrace my inner Desert more these days.

I don't talk about it much, but I've been burnt out on writing fiction for a long time. I haven't even started a fiction project in almost a year. Every time I do, I suffer debilitating panic attacks.

To help me get back on the horse, I'm working with my agent to identify genres I can write well, that are highly saleable, and don't take a lot of my emotional labor to finish. Hopefully, divesting the work from my emotional connection to it will allow me to move forward in a way I haven't been able to in a while.

Let me be clear, ***I care deeply about doing a good job with all of this stuff.*** It's just that my whole essence isn't wrapped up in other people liking it or not, and that frees me up to find even bigger and better hits.

I'm trying to be better about finding hits in top genres now. Even when I'm writing in my favorite genre of portal fantasy, I'm trying to think of ways to optimize my work to find the most readers. These days I'm combining my Tundra ability to launch well with a Desert's natural instinct to find large pockets of fans and deliver a satisfying experience to them, amplifying both skills to take my career to a new level.

While everyone has an ecosystem where they feel the most comfortable, most successful authors will eventually reach a point where they must evolve beyond their natural state to achieve the success they crave.

This need to evolve also makes it difficult to analyze the ecosystems of very successful authors because they incorporate aspects of different ecosystems into their businesses.

Brené Brown is probably a natural Grassland. Her work is grounded in systems thinking. She builds clear, repeatable frameworks and constructs an evergreen content ecosystem around them. Her books interlink. Her talks cross-reference her research. Her backlist compounds over time. That's textbook Grassland.

But what makes her unforgettable is her Forest-style delivery that's intimate, emotionally vulnerable, and voice-forward. She shows up with her whole self and gives readers permission to do the same.

This is how ecosystems work in the real world. Brené didn't choose between reach and resonance. She structured her scale (Grassland) around her emotional brand (Forest) and built one of the most powerful, sustainable platforms in nonfiction today.

It's very hard to be an uber-successful author without evolving beyond your natural ecosystem, but it's also critical that you know your natural ecosystem, because when all the chips are down, you will revert back to your natural state in order to regroup and regain your balance.

I have started so many businesses that eventually failed, or that I shuttered, that it's staggering. There's one thing about failure we don't talk about a lot.

The time you spent doing the thing you failed at has real, tangible value.

I recently shuttered my Verizon dealership after nearly 10 years. It used to account for as much as 80% of my revenue, but those days are long gone.

Those years where it carried my business have value. The relationships I made running it have value. The skills I built running that business have value. Most importantly, the money I made during that time had value.

People often only want to try new things when they are sure they'll be successful, *but some things only serve you for a season*.

That season, though, it might save your life. Additionally, the time you spent doing that task might have immense financial value in another season.

I stopped running book marketing in 2021 because it didn't serve me, but then a year later an opportunity I couldn't deny came up that fit perfectly. Now, that one client makes me more money per month than my other sources combined.

Twenty years ago, I was a substitute teacher. I hadn't been in a classroom in over a decade, but last year I brushed off the rust and started substitute teaching to get me through a rough patch. *I have no shame about doing any type of work when things get rough or if I think it will serve me, even if it only lasts for a month.*

The Author Stack sells courses and non-fiction books, but it's not my first time doing that work. In fact, I licensed all my work to Monica in 2020 because my previous attempts were miserable failures. I never thought I would do non-fiction again after that.

Look at me now. *We've made more in the past year than I did in all my previous attempts at this combined.* Those years I spent building those old businesses had value, even after I gave it up, and they helped me succeed years later. I made tens of thousands of dollars on those "failed" businesses before I shuttered them.

That Verizon dealership came from a partnership that blew up in my face, but I was left with the means to carry my business for years.

This also happens in fiction. My best-selling series was an abysmal failure when I first launched it, but retooling and relaunching it on Kickstarter brought new life to it. Now, that series is the lynchpin of my whole fiction business.

Somebody once told me that 99 out of 100 businesses won't make it past 10 years, but 99 out of 100 people make it past 40, which means people had rich lives before that business and after it. That resonates with me deeply.

Just because those businesses failed doesn't mean the years they spent running them didn't have value. ***They served their owner until they didn't, and that's okay.*** You can have a deep, meaningful life even if something fails. It can mean a lot to you even if you decide to give it up.

It's not that failure is a life lesson. ***You get more out of even failure than just a lesson.*** Sometimes, you get a lifeline. Other times you plant the seed for success in the future. Most times, it gives you enough money to survive until the next thing.

Even if all you get is clarity on what you don't want to do with your life, that time has way more value than we give it credit for, especially financially.

All three of my main sources of income are built upon the burnt ashes of businesses that failed. Even before they failed though, they served me…just for a season, not my whole life.

CHAPTER 10

HOW EACH AUTHOR ECOSYSTEM THINKS ABOUT AND USES TRENDS

One of the most interesting ways to parse The Author Ecosystems is how each type deals with trends in the marketplace. Just like the easiest way for me to tell your Enneagram is by seeing what you default to in stress, one of the most decisive ways to learn an author's ecosystem is to find out how they think about trends in the market and how it relates to their author business.

Depending on your ecosystem, one of these will likely resonate above the others and should give you an insight into how you build your author business. It should also give you insight into how the other ecosystems think about their own author business to give you opportunities to evolve.

Remember, the goal of every ecosystem is to evolve and incorporate all five ecosystems into their business. However, before we can do that we need to find one line of business that works for us and resonates above the others. If you're struggling to find success, it's probably because the way you build your books is in direct contradiction to how your ecosystem thinks about trends.

DESERT – TREND RIDING

A Desert is deep in the thick of their genre, gobbling up precious reader data in Facebook groups, sitting in silence and taking notes as they watch how the industry is flowing so they can accurately predict the next trend and ride it like a wave.

Deserts are experts in knowing when a trend is losing its arbitrage and have the preternatural ability to catch the next trend before too many authors saturate the market.

I define arbitrage as the **difference, or delta**, between **supply** and **demand**. When there is **more** demand than supply, then there is an arbitrage opportunity. The higher the arbitrage the more a Desert can milk that opportunity before the gap closes…

…and that gap will always close. Authors will always, given enough time, find the pockets of underserved readers and start writing for them, if for no other reason than because K-lytics exists to do this work for authors. Their entire business model is about showing authors emerging categories where the demand for a type of book exceeds the supply of them.

A Desert is simply conscious enough to recognize when the tides turn. If you're not a Desert, you'll probably enter a market well after the trend has peaked and you won't be able to write fast enough to take advantage of the next one, either.

GRASSLAND – TREND WEAVING

Grasslands highly value data just like Deserts, but instead of looking at the current trends, they are trying to peg an emerging trend 1-2 years down the road and move the industry toward that north star on the horizon. A great example of this is Monica Leonelle, who recognized the industry trend toward direct sales years ago and started to create content that buoyed our company to take advantage of them when those trends emerged. Along the way, she wrote about other things, but by the time direct sales became a hot topic, we already had several books on the subject and were able to become a go-to source for information.

For a Grassland to stay relevant in the short term, they practice trend weaving, which allows them to take hot trends and thread them into their existing topic. While a Desert will hit a trend perfectly, a Grassland hits a trend at 90% of perfect because they are always trying to steer the conversation toward that topic.

An unhealthy Grassland will see a trend on the horizon and lose focus on how to weave their topic together with what's happening currently to build relevancy until people are ready to talk about that topic.

I got a ton of blank stares for talking about Kickstarter back in 2015, well before the trend was even a blip on the horizon. Meanwhile, Monica was able to weave Kickstarter and direct sales into the prevailing narrative of the industry and make people care, so that by the time the Brandon Sanderson campaign raised $41 million we were positioned as the only expert with a book on the topic, and were able to leverage that into major opportunities.

TUNDRA – TREND STACKING

Tundras love to stack evergreen tropes and seasonal trends on top of each other, making an irresistible package that turns every eye in an industry when they launch a book. They aren't concerned with current or future trends. They are looking for trends that stand the test of time.

I made a huge error when moving my Godsverse Chronicle graphic novels into novels because the trends that worked at conventions or even in comics weren't the same as the ones present in the book market. The first books I wrote (*Death, Doom, Hell,* and *Ruin*) missed the mark so badly that I wrote four new novels (*Magic, Evil, Time,* and *Heaven*) to slot in before them to help better hit those trends in the book market that I missed. I additionally had to change the titles and covers multiple times as I learned the market better and how to signal correctly to readers. *Death* started as *Katrina Hates Everything* before it became *The Gods' Sin,* then *Death Followed Behind Her* until it finally became *Death* and got a new cover treatment. Before that, it was a series of three short novellas at a time well before short reads were in vogue.

I learned the evergreen tropes in fantasy were dragons and fairy tales (and to a lesser extent mythology), so my next series, *The Obsidian Spindle Saga,* featured them both prominently, and I never had to change the titles (though I did redesign the covers for their retail release).

As the name suggests, Tundras are experts at seasonal launches that take into account the trends of a season. They are not looking to capitalize on a trend the first time through. Instead, they're looking for a trend that has come around multiple times so they can capitalize when it comes around again. They are great at feeling the "vibes" and knowing when to launch for maximum impact and visibility.

For instance, I was the one who told Monica to drop everything so we could make The Kickstarter Accelerator happen right after Sanderson's campaign ended. While Monica knew the trend was coming, I was able to know when the fervor was at its zenith.

Tundras often write 1-2 years ahead of their slate and sit on books until the vibes are right to strike. They use a combination of data, gut instinct, and seasonal buying behavior to plan their promotional calendar and sit right between the data-heavy ecosystems (Deserts and Grasslands) and the gut-heavy ecosystems (Forests and Aquatics) in how they think about trends.

FOREST – TREND TWISTING

Forests seem to think that their ecosystem justifies writing any and every weird thing they want and that by holding onto their unique energy they will eventually break through and have success due to sheer force of will alone, but that's not quite true.

Yes, you need to listen to your gut more than other ecosystems, but a healthy Forest is very interested in trends. However, they are most interested in using existing trends and twisting them in a way that resonates with their readers in a different way than any of the ecosystems we mentioned above.

One example we learned about recently was a successful author who took the trope of the "***alphahole***" and asked, "What if instead of the leader of this shifter wolf pack was a jerk like I've read dozens of times, they worked more like a real wolf pack and all worked lovingly together?"

That twist takes a popular trope and gives it a specific twist that long-time fans will enjoy. ***They don't write satire.*** They deeply love their genre, read broadly in it, and twist those tropes lovingly in ways that will delight readers. Too often people poke fun at genres they don't like in books and that never works. Readers hate being insulted, but many can appreciate the flaws in their genre when they see them highlighted.

Forests should target their books to readers who have read broadly and understand the "canon" of a genre so they can appreciate the unique spin an author brings to the genre. Because of this, Forests can enter a genre late and have success, while Deserts almost always need to be at the front of a trend, setting the pace and the reader expectations Forests will twist.

One reason a Forest writes in so many different genres is because they find similar themes and tropes they can twist in different places. While a Grassland is loyal to a topic, a Forest is loyal to their themes, which is why their fans more than any other type will read anything they do. They aren't reading the genre. They are reading the theme.

AQUATIC- TREND MAKING

Then you have the Aquatic, over in the corner making their own trend from scratch and building slowly over time to craft their thriving fanbase for their universe. However, they can learn a lot from the above ecosystems by taking hot trends and weaving them into their universe or twisting a trend in a way that brings in new readers.

In tech, there are five types of adopters: **innovators, early adopters, the early majority, the late majority, and laggards**. Each one of these has different buying habits and reasons for joining. The innovators are usually buying something because it's new and exciting. Show them something new, like your universe, and they will buy just for the kitsch of it, but there are few of them compared to the other types. Aquatics tend to stick pretty close to the innovators, who supported them early, but in order to grow they need to move through the adopter stages by varying their output.

The classic example we use is *Star Wars*, which is so clearly an Aquatic franchise. Not only did George Lucas bring in new formats with books, action figures, and other merchandise, but more recently Kathleen Kennedy started using hot trends to bring in new fans. *The Mandalorian* is a very simple space western that appeals to a very different viewership than *A New Hope*. Every new TV series is a chance to bring in new fans. Marvel has started to do much the same thing, which makes sense since they are both owned by the same company and are both targeting the majority (both early and late) who make up most of their fans.

My friend wrote a cozy mystery series into their existing fantasy world to capture new readers and give new ways to hook people. Aquatics are very concerned with expanding into different modalities, but they can find a lot of value in writing into different areas to make their universe relatable to more people.

THE ECOSYSTEM TREND CYCLE

One of the most interesting parts about the Author Ecosystems is what we're calling the "Trend Cycle", which looks like this:

- **Aquatics** start doing something interesting that gets traction with an audience.
- **Grasslands** notice that traction and start trying to figure out what is happening. Once they have it figured out, they start moving the industry toward it.
- **Deserts** see the massive arbitrage in a trend and start building the market for it until it finds equilibrium.
- **Tundras** seek out the evergreen trope in a trend and maximize it for profit and efficiency.
- **Forests** enter a mature market and twist stale trends to breathe new life into them.
- **Aquatics** start the cycle again.

What's interesting about this is how it plays with the technology adoption curve that starts with innovators, then moves to early adopters, the early majority, the late majority, and finally the laggards pulling up the rear.

What this tells us is that Aquatics and Forests are both next to each other and on very different ends of that curve. It seems like Forests and Aquatics are next to each other, but Aquatics are really at the start of a new trend ***and*** the back end of an existing trend.

The reason Aquatics end up on either end of this curve is because their job is to find the point of improvement in any trend and pull them together into something new. A classic example is Southwest, which took dozens of problems in the industry and fixed them all at once, creating an ecosystem that couldn't be replicated by anyone else. They only have a fractional share of the market, but those who use them are incredibly loyal.

Another great example is Apple, which for decades only had a 1-2% fractional share of the market, but because of how they integrated everything in a novel way they had loyal fans and no competition could replicate them.

Even though these were massively innovative companies, both Southwest and Apple took advantage of burgeoning markets to build around that took off. If they didn't have the market rising behind them, the trend they created would have fizzled and, likely, died.

In books, we think of somebody like Cassandra Clare, who took Twilight, along with Supernatural suspense and mythology, and created something brand new, or an author like RJ Blain, who combined paranormal romance, romantic comedy, mystery, and thriller together in a way nobody had thought of before and now owns the category of "Magical Romantic Comedy…with a body count."

Something else that this tells us is that Forests often enter markets too early, and Deserts need to exit markets before they hit that equilibrium. Meanwhile, Tundras are probably right in the middle, trying to time the market when excitement is at its peak. Deserts exiting a market should be a bellwether that it's time to launch imminently.

It's important to note this has nothing to do with how Deserts think of fandom. They are still trying to hit the middle of the market, but they want to enter a market when fewer people know about it, specifically fewer authors who know about it to drown readers with a flood of supply.

Aquatics generally create categories and then benefit from the whole rest of the adoption curve. All the good things point back to them, but if it doesn't catch they will likely crash and burn. Then, *Grasslands* should enter in the Innovator/Early Adopter phase. *Deserts* should enter during the Early Adopter/Early Majority phase, *Tundras* should enter right at the zenith between Early and Late Majority before interest wanes, and *Forests* should enter in the Late Majority into mature markets.

Forests, *more than any other ecosystem*, are prone to see a trend and leap on it before the tropes are commonplace and when that happens their habit of twisting tropes brings confusion. If you look at the fantasy category, today's series builds upon J.R.R. Tolkien, mythology, and everything that came before to make those tropes commonplace. Once the majority of people in a genre know the tropes, then your twists will be delightful instead of befuddling.

Grasslands, then, should spend a lot of time searching out Aquatics who are doing novel things, and Deserts should draft from Grasslands to find new upcoming trends.

Meanwhile, Tundras should wait to enter a market until it's at its peak, which is something the movie industry tries to track to time their releases.

FINAL THOUGHTS

It feels from this analysis that Deserts and Grasslands almost need to go first into a trend to set the tropes. Once they've established the tone, timber, and tropes of how to write a book that fans will love and resonate with, a Tundra can analyze the evergreen tropes and Forests can twist those tropes to find new and interesting ways into their theme.

Perhaps even an Aquatic needs to set the trend by developing it from nothing into something viable before the Desert gets there. Then, the Desert picks up on something interesting and starts to build out the tropes until the category is mature, attracting the other ecosystems to join.

If that's true, then one of the reasons a Forest wouldn't be successful moving into a new trope too soon is because the category isn't mature enough to have the tropes become a shared language between readers, and thus the twist the Forests give to those tropes confuses readers instead of delights them. Additionally, while it seems that Aquatics and Deserts are at opposite poles, they might have a more symbiotic relationship than previously thought, with Aquatics breathing life into a new subcategory and Deserts stabilizing it in kind.

One of the easiest ways to get healthy in your ecosystem is the stick closely to how it maximizes the value of both long-term and short-term trends. If you are a Desert, maybe don't twist that trope because your subgenre isn't ready for that yet. One reason Forests do well in established genres is because they are playing upon the shared language of the community. Until people have a base understanding of how tropes work, twisting them doesn't resonate as well. Once a market is saturated, then people are looking for new twists on older stories.

In the same way, Tundras traffic in excitement, so launching that series before interest is at a fervor won't do you any favors. Other ecosystems trying to get to #1 in the Amazon store fail to recognize that Tundras drop new releases into a hungry audience, once the trend has come back around. They aren't looking to stay ahead of a trend because they know if they wait, the trend will emerge again. Then, they will be ready to capitalize, and why if they aren't using evergreen tropes their work will be in vain.

If you're ready to evolve, trying to incorporate these different methods of engagement can fast-track your growth. Once you understand how each ecosystem deals with trends, it makes it easier to dissect their launches and find the special sauce that works for them, and how to bring that into your own business.

CHAPTER 11

BUILDING A TEAM USING AUTHOR ECOSYSTEMS

When authors start learning about the Author Ecosystems, they generally map it onto their own experience to learn about themselves, but our system is equally powerful in building out a team around your work. Whether you're working by yourself, co-writing with a partner, working in a shared world, building an anthology, expanding your business with a small team, or developing a full publishing slate, the author ecosystem can help you grow your business.

We've already talked extensively about the evolution path for every ecosystem, including how to identify ecosystems in other people for the sake of your personal growth, but not everyone wants to embrace every ecosystem inside themselves. Many authors would prefer to hire for different positions inside their business, and we think that's great. It's probably essential to hire beyond yourself to succeed as an author.

At Wannabe Press, being able to identify the qualities we need in a role and map them onto a specific ecosystem, then hire somebody in that ecosystem, has revolutionized our hiring practices. We know that we don't do everything well. For instance, Monica and I are dreadful Forests. That might seem kind of incredible since The Author

Ecosystems is an intrinsically Forest-based shared language and culture system, but we're not good at engaging with fans or fostering that culture in any of our businesses.

Instead, we looked for people to partner with who fill in our deficiencies. Mel Jolly and Tawdra Kandle, the conference directors for our previous Writer MBA conference, are both incredible Forests with heavy Aquatic tendencies. They are great at the engage and delight areas of the flywheel that we laid out previously. Meanwhile, Monica and I are great at the Attract stage of the flywheel and in building a sales funnel. Monica can embrace her inner Desert through analyzing data, a natural skill of a Grassland, and I can build out the top of the funnel by starting at the bottom and working up, a natural strength of a Tundra.

This is a graphic showing the strength of each ecosystem in the funnel/flywheel model.

Even though we would love to hire a Desert who was naturally great at those aspects, our biggest deficits have been in the Forest and Aquatic bits of our business, which is where Mel and Tawdra shine.

So, let's talk about how to use the Author Ecosystems to build out a team inside your business. This is one of the few times where you will find us breaking from our normal format of talking about the ecosystems in the standard Desert, Grassland, Tundra, Forest, Aquatic order. I think it's more important to visualize these positions when they would be relevant to your business instead of how we've been talking about them so far.

Before I get to it, I want to state that if you work in one of these roles and aren't the ecosystem we recommend seeking out for that task, it doesn't make you bad at your job. There are aspects of every ecosystem that can help in each of these roles, and you might be great at embracing bits of an ecosystem that is not your own. This is only a thought exercise.

HIRE 1: EDITORIAL

Almost every author's first hire will be an editor, whether that's a developmental editor, a copy editor, or a proofreader.

In this role, you'll likely be looking for somebody detail-oriented who can hold a lot of disparate threads in their head at any one time. An editor's job is to make sure everything flows properly and makes sense as a cohesive whole. Because of this, the ideal person for this role is a Grassland, whose superpower is depth.

We believe this is why most anthologies and shared world projects fail. These types of projects are almost always proposed by Forests, who want to build community and shared language through collaboration, and they fall apart either because those Forests misjudge the market or because they have no interest in making sure everything fits as one cohesive whole. Additionally, Forests attract a lot of Forests, who don't like writing to spec and thus all the stories are wildly off the mark.

Grasslands, with their ability to forecast the future and deep-seated interest in intricate detail, are perfect for this role in any organization. If you're hiring at a publishing company, look for Grasslands to fill your EIC roles and plan out your content calendar. Grasslands are also great at predicting cover trends and making sure you're meeting the market where it will be in 18-24 months when your books launch.

HIRE 2: COMMUNITY MANAGEMENT

Once you've had some success, the next place authors usually turn to for help is in community management. Since half the industry is filled with Deserts, Grasslands, and Tundras who are generally uninterested in community above writing new stories for them, this makes sense. Some authors have a natural affinity for community and fostering engagement with their readers, and those kinds of people are going to be equally good at helping you build your community.

It should be no surprise that we think Forests are perfect for this role. These are the people who love to dig deep with fans and create posts specifically for fan engagement instead of growth. They are masters at getting people to open up and construct a community in a way that feels like a safe space.

Aside from Forests and Aquatics, the other Ecosystems are most interested in growth above engagement, and you really need to pick one or the other as your target.

One of the things I learned by hiring my own engagement people is that engagement requires completely rewiring your brain to write posts that foster that kind of community. You can't just put "Leave us a comment" in a post and expect engagement. With The Author Stack, I can tell which articles are going to have high engagement before they get out the door.

Ironically, these are often the articles with the lowest overall readership, but they'll have 10x the comments of another article even though fewer people read it. I've tried hard to write the kinds of articles that get tons of engagement and I'm just not good at it. It's a skill deeply embedded into the writing process, which is one reason Forests also make good editors. They will bring that out of your work and make you feel seen in the process. However, if you have a deeply complex world, they are less good at holding all of it in their head than focusing on really great character interactions that resonate with your readers.

HIRE 3: ADS MANAGEMENT

The biggest mistake writers make when building a team is hiring the same person to handle their community and their ads. I have been running ads for years and the only constant has been that the ads with the best engagement are *never* the ones that get the most sales conversion.

If you want sales from your ads, it's best not to hire a Forest to run them. Because so many authors hire for community first, the vast majority of VAs are Forests. Authors see how well they do in one aspect of their business and try to jam them into another part they hate, namely advertising, with disastrous results.

That's because ads require a ton of optimizations and data analysis, which goes against every strength of a Forest, so they almost always struggle with ads. Deserts, on the other hand, are amazing at ads management (as are Grasslands) because they love digging into the data. Additionally, they will know what's hot right now, because they follow that type of thing, and stay on top of how to get the most out of your ad spend.

Deserts also make amazing cover designers because they are not swayed by a community or even their author clients. They are locked into following what's hot in the market right now. For this reason, if you have a Desert cover designer, do not engage them until very late in the process, because they are going to give you a cover that's hot at the moment. If you hold it for years, your cover won't reflect those trends and your book will suffer for it.

The one constant thing we see in advertising is that you should absolutely not hire your Forest VA to run your ads, even if they are amazing at running your community. Hire a Desert or a Grassland to run your ads, or help foster your VA to evolve their Desert energy to help you, but don't expect them to be great out of the gate.

HIRE 4: LAUNCH TEAM

Eventually, your author business will grow to the point where you're capping out at what you can earn with ad optimizations and community management alone, and want to bring on somebody to help you launch better. That might mean getting to #1 in the store, packaging your books so people spend more money, or planning your pre-launch more effectively to maximize excitement.

This is where a Tundra can help you. By the time you get to this point, you've probably got a slamming series, with an engaged community, and your ads are profitable. Now, you need to expand your profit and bring more attention to every launch, and Tundras traffic in excitement. They can help you put together a more powerful offer for your series that will get the attention of the industry, and help you take advantage of every day of your launch.

These are the PR consultants who craft your sales pitch so it's as enticing to as many people as possible. These are the editors that you bring on to help you incorporate more evergreen trends and tropes into your work for maximum effectiveness. Tundras can really help with a "USA Today list run", if those even exist anymore, to get you a lot of exposure and sales in a concentrated timeframe. If you've been writing in relative obscurity and you are ready to get noticed, or especially if you are launching a Kickstarter, you want a Tundra on your team.

HIRE 5: BRAND EXPANSION

Now that you're rocking and rolling, having piqued the interest of the industry and shown you have a viable brand, you'll want to expand outside of books into other modalities, and this is where an Aquatic can be especially helpful.

It usually takes them a long time to get their own brand built from scratch, but they can be like gasoline on the fire of a successful business because they naturally understand the different areas where you can expand your brand. Whether it's into new platforms or new formats, Aquatics always seem to know the important players and have relationships they can leverage to grow your business quickly. You might not think of hiring an Aquatic because their business is usually small until it explodes, but their minds work in a way very different from the average author and they can be an invaluable addition to your team.

Additionally, many successful authors want to hold events or special offers to delight their fans, and Aquatics are masters of this type of delight. They are walking bundles of joy to fans because they are always looking for ways to delight them with something new. This is why they have the highest brand loyalty of any ecosystem.

FINAL THOUGHTS

No matter your ecosystem, partnering with people in other ecosystems can help you grow. Whenever I go onto a podcast hosted by a Forest, I can almost always make it their most watched episode because I bring the excitement, while their articles on my publication almost always have incredible engagement, helping build loyalty to what I'm doing on my own.

As a Tundra, I often partner with successful authors to give their launches a boost, and implementing my strategies usually gives them the best launch of my career, and better than I can do on my own.

It wasn't until Monica, a Grassland, and me, a Tundra, built a company together that we got the kind of traction either of us wanted, and bringing in universally loved Forests and Aquatics like Mel and Tawdra made everyone want to work with us because they already wanted to work with them.

While we should all be working to evolve ourselves, expanding business almost always means looking outside ourselves and partnering or hiring with other ecosystems to get where we want to go.

CHAPTER 12

HOW TO BUILD A SALES FUNNEL AND FLYWHEEL USING AUTHOR ECOSYSTEMS

The heart of any business is the sales and marketing engine. Companies run on money, after all. It's what they burn to keep going, and so creating an engine that at least breaks even every year is how we ensure that we keep going for the long haul.

There are two main parts of a sales and marketing engine: the sales funnel and the flywheel. They both work in concert with each other, but they are distinct concepts, and different Author Ecosystems will resonate with each piece of it.

WHAT IS A SALES FUNNEL?

Very few customers will ever close on a deal the day you meet them. Customers need time to get to know you, like you, and build trust with you before they buy your product or service. ***What you do today is predictive of your success in six to eight weeks.***

That's right.

Your hard work today won't pay off for nearly two months. This is what hampers many artists from growing their businesses. **They give up before they can ever**

realistically succeed. We live in a world of instant gratification, and success in business is a long-term payoff. Over time, your hard work compounds through the success of your sales funnel.

A sales funnel is no different than a funnel you would use in your kitchen or to put oil into your car: wide at the top with a narrow bottom. Into the top of the funnel goes potential customers and out the bottom comes clients. It's as simple as that.

There are five stages in my sales funnel. The first stage is that people need to know you exist. This is called *the Awareness stage*.

At this stage of the funnel, you aren't trying to find the right clients. You are simply looking for as many potential customers as possible. The rest of the funnel will weed out people who are bad matches for your product, and leave you only with perfect fits. You need to cast the widest net possible at this stage, because the wider the top of the funnel becomes, the wider it will be at the bottom.

Let's assume you need to talk to one hundred people in order to find one client. If you only talk to twenty people a month, you will not find a new client for five months. In this case, by simply talking to five times more people, you can find a client every month. If you increase that to two or three hundred people a month, you can find two to three clients a month. This alone can exponentially increase your revenue.

The second stage of the funnel is getting people to like you. This is called *the Consideration stage.*

This is when we start narrowing the funnel down. We need to push out content that is attractive to our ideal client, whether that means sharing comic book pages, short stories, or articles about pandas.

Whatever you share, it should be hyper-targeted to your ideal client. If it is, then people who are interested in the things you are sharing will grow to like you. Meanwhile, people who aren't interested will drop out of your funnel before you invest too much energy in them.

This is the stage where people fall out of your funnel the most. You shouldn't be nervous when people unfollow you or unsubscribe from your mailing list at this point. My mailing list has a 31 percent unsubscribe rate in the first couple of weeks of somebody joining. I love that number because it means I'm weeding out the people who don't care about what I do.

This process of showing people what you do, building empathy with your ideal client, and weeding out ones who don't care about your message is one of the most powerful tools in business. Unfortunately, because of our natural need to be liked, we shy away from offending anybody. As a result, we try to please everybody and thus attract nobody.

Weeding out people who don't fit your product is a natural part of business. You shouldn't care about those people anyway, because they won't buy from you. Heck, they don't even like you. Your job isn't to please people who have no interest in what you are doing with your business. Your job is to connect with as many people as possible and let the right ones self-select to be part of your network over the long haul.

The third stage of the funnel is making people trust you. This is called ***the Decision, or Purchase, stage.***

This is the trickiest part of the funnel. Everybody left at this stage of the funnel is in your ideal customer pool. Now, you have to convince them to buy your product. Even within your ideal client pool, there will be people who don't like your specific take and won't buy.

Take a car for instance. Even among car buyers, some people want the most reliable vehicle for their family, others want a sports car with the fastest engine. Still, others want the most luxurious ride on the road.

That's why car companies have multiple brands and models. There are many features people might want, and it's critical to target the right message to the right customer. If we didn't have different needs, then everybody would be driving around in the same beige Honda Accord, right?

But we aren't driving around in the same cars. There are more than a hundred different types of cars on the road, all with different features, sold by different companies, under different brands. They all capture a different part of the market. They all speak to a different type of person.

The same is true with your product. If you create high-end geek chic necklaces that cost $100 or more, then you are isolating yourself from people who are looking for cheap charms, and isolating yourself even more from people looking for an art print, or a comic book.

That's natural. That's good. Heck, that's necessary to create a sustainable business. This is what finding the right client for your product is all about.

The fourth stage of the funnel is making your customer happy. You have proven you are the right person to help them. Hooray! You've got a customer. Now we have to keep them happy so they buy again. This is called *the Retention stage*.

Notice there are three stages in this funnel before buying your product even comes into the equation. There will be people in your funnel who know you but won't like you, like you but won't trust you, and trust you but won't buy from you.

We can see this play out in our own lives. We all have a coworker we hate but can't get rid of, or a family member we love but wouldn't trust with a dollar of our money. We all have those people in our lives, but we also have a friend we would gladly give money to because we know they'll use our money to do something awesome.

The same is true with your business. Most people won't buy from you. When I go to a convention, I'm lucky if one percent of people sign up for my mailing list and 10 percent of those people ever buy from me. Even at a convention like San Diego Comic-Con, where I make thousands of dollars, I only sell a few hundred books and there are over 160,000 people in attendance.

T*hat's okay.* In fact, that's how a funnel is supposed to work. This year we were set up in the small press area of San Diego Comic-Con, which meant people who came down our aisle self-identified as people who liked independent comic books. That already narrowed the field of potential customers down quite a bit.

From there, all I had to do was engage with as many people as possible so that some of them would like me, and some of those people would trust me, and then some of those people would buy from me.

In the end, by knowing how many people would attend the event, I could accurately predict how much I would make, and next year I can make an even more accurate prediction because I have even more data. This is the power of the funnel. If you understand how it works, you can predict the revenue for your entire business months into the future.

The final stage is about building evangelists who will tell other people about your work. The absolute best marketing comes from word of mouth. When other people talk about your work to their friends, it's much easier to get others to buy than from your own marketing efforts. This is called **the Advocacy stage**.

This can include providing referral links, building a strong community, offering giveaways to readers, or generally showering them with love. Most importantly, it involves creating mind-blowing products people can't help but talk about with other people. This is called network effects.

This is not an effect contained to your buyers, either. One of the best ways to generate network effects is among other creators doing interesting work. You can create a recommendation network through platforms like Substack, Sparkloop, or Beehiiv to cross-promote with other creators.

This cross-promotion feature provides a way for writers to promote and discover each other on their own terms. A quick story about network effects, and how when one creator wins the whole network wins. Substack spotlighted and interviewed Laura Kennedy from Peak Notions.

I love Laura's work, so I was rooting for her really hard when I read it, but throughout the day I noticed I was getting dozens of free subscribers to my Substack.

I usually get 20-30 a day, so I was very confused about getting 60+ in just a couple of hours. It took me a while to think, "Wait, doesn't Laura recommend The Author Stack?"

So, I checked and her publication had sent me 50 recommendations that day. Laura ended up getting 1,500+ subscribers from that article, and I received over 100 because she recommended my publication. You never know where those surges will come from, but they can be powerful if you set them up properly.

I have over 100 publications recommending mine, and I recommend a bunch, too. Every month I get 300-500 from it and everyone else gets a bit from me I hope. Nobody needs to do the bulk of the work when everyone is working together.

There is one more point I want to make before ending this section. When you start selling your work, a small number of people will buy from you immediately. This is because you have spent decades building up trust with certain people in your life. Those people have already worked their way to the bottom of your funnel and are ready to make a buying decision the moment you launch your storefront. Once those people work their way through the bottom of your funnel, though, there won't be anybody left to buy your product if you haven't built out the top of your funnel properly.

I've seen far too many creatives tell me that lots of people bought their book in the first month of release, but they haven't seen another sale for over a year. This happens because they relied on their existing network to buy their product initially, and once those people flushed out of their funnel there was nobody to replace them. Remember, a funnel is only as good as the number of people you put into the top of it.

Today, we'll be talking about three different areas of funnels, and how they map to the stages I mentioned above.

They are **BOFU (Bottom Of FUnnel),** which deals with the **Decision** stage, **TOFU (Top Of FUnnel)**, which deals with the **Awareness** stage, and **MOFU (Middle Of FUnnel)**, which deals with the **Consideration** stage.

I have listed them out of order because we'll be talking about them out of order for reasons that will hopefully become clear. Once we finish up with funnels, we'll be talking about flywheels, which deal with the **After Purchase** stages of **Retention** and **Advocacy**, and how they relate to attracting, engaging, and delighting your readers.

BOFU - BOTTOM OF FUNNEL

Which ecosystem is the best at this part? Tundras

Tundras traffic in excitement and that excitement is packaged in the offers they present to their audience. It's not enough to just present something to your readers.

No, *you have to make it irresistible if you want them to take advantage of it.* Tundras excel is creating irresistible offers.

That's something all the other ecosystems gloss over. They often believe that by simply offering something their readers will buy, but the reason they are busy is intrinsically locked inside the power of the offer. *The better the offer, the more people will buy.* If you have the right offer, then you can sell anything to anyone.

There are two levers you can pull to make something irresistible.

- **Adding more to the offer.** This doesn't mean adding just anything to an offer, though. It means adding to an offer to make it more "complete", whatever that means to your reader. I try to create at least 2x value with every offer, meaning that *if the elements of an offer sell for $50 at retail, I will sell it for no more than $25 when I package it in an offer.*
- **Lowering the price of the offer.** This one is pretty easy. If you cut the cost of your offer, it becomes more appealing. In general, *I try to give at least 2x value in an offer, but if I can get more, I will do*

it. The more value you pack into an offer, the more irresistible it becomes.

On top of that, you need to layer on some psychological, or buying, triggers to help make your offer even more appealing. There are six essential buying triggers that have stood the test of time. They work in any creative field with any set of potential customers.

- **Commitment** – When somebody willingly commits to joining your community, they are more likely to buy your product. This is the main value to people joining your mailing list, or wearing a button, or even taking a flier. They make a commitment when performing that action. It signifies they are part of your community. The more actions they take, the more commitment they build. Every time they open a newsletter from you and don't unsubscribe, they are affirming that commitment. Every time they like one of your tweets or share a Facebook post, they are affirming their commitment to your brand again and again. The more you can enforce that commitment through words and actions, the more likely you are to have an enthusiastic ambassador for your brand, one who buys all your stuff.
- **Reciprocity** – When you do something nice for somebody, they want to help you. That's just human nature. Knowing this, you need to provide value for your potential customer before you ever ask for a sale. Once you have provided incredible value through advice or some sort of free content, then people will gladly give you money, because you have helped them and treated them like a human being.

- **Social Proof** – Human beings want to be part of the "in" crowd. If you can prove that other people are using your product, everybody else will want to use it, too. The hardest sales to make at conventions are the first ones. Once there are people running around the show floor with your product, other people are more likely to want it, as well. Your work becomes valuable to a customer because other people saw the value in it already. People want to buy what their peers bought. They don't want to be left out in the cold. If you can show your customer that people they like and respect use your product, then you are more likely to convince them to buy it, too.

- **Scarcity** – When you limit the available quantity of a product, customers become increasingly likely to make a buying decision in the moment. People believe products will be around forever and that they can always buy it later. When they realize a product is in limited supply, they are forced to make an immediate decision. This works wonders for people sitting on the fence about buying your product and also for people who desperately want your product but need a little push to finally take action.

- **Authority** – If you can demonstrate you are an expert in your field, people are more likely to buy your product over somebody else's. This is how you stand out above every other creative doing exactly what you do. They choose you because you are an expert in your field. To prove your expertise, it's important to have consistently high-selling products for a long time, and it helps if you're able to teach other people how to do what you do. Another way is to write guest posts on other blogs, share your work on podcasts, or speak on panels. You can also use platforms like Medium and Kickstarter to build expertise, as the platform's authority can be transferred to you.

- **Liking** – If somebody has a positive connection to you, they are more likely to buy from you. Think about it: You are more inclined to buy from somebody you like than somebody you don't care about, right? Of course you are.

The success or failure of your funnel is decided when you package your offer together. If you want to see how I designed a series offer for my Godsverse Chronicles series, then you can find it at
https://russellnohelty.com/godsversecompletesales

You'll notice I packaged my whole 12-book series together, and then offered it at 60% off retail. However, this is a one-time offer that disappears when the countdown timer hits zero, effectively using the scarcity buying trigger. Additionally, I have a bump offer to include the audiobooks and audio commentary for a total of $50, and then an upsell to get all of my novels for $100.

These offers are called profit maximizers.

Because you aren't getting the same volume from direct sales as you are from retailers, your goal should be about maximizing the cart value of every sale. One of the most important metrics in direct sales is average cart value.

Basically, when you sell somebody one thing, you want to sell them more things. At the moment of purchase, customers enter "buyer mode" where they are the most suggestible to spend more.

At this point, we want to offer more value to them through cross-sells, upsells, downsells, and bump offers.

A *cross-sell* is when you offer a wholly different, but complementary product or format to your audience after a sale. So, for instance, if you are selling a bag of chips, a cross-sell could ask customers to buy a tub of salsa to complete the experience. With books, cross-selling could be offering a different series to "complete their library" or offering audiobooks to your customers purchasing ebooks.

An *upsell* is selling a more expensive version of the same product. So, if you are selling paperback books, offering people a "hardcover upgrade" would be an upsell. Additionally, offering "special edition ebooks" instead of the standard ebooks would be an upsell. Additionally, you can offer more books in the same series as an upsell, as well.

A *downsell* is initialed when a cross-sell or upsell doesn't work. Usually, an upsell or cross-sell should be 3-5x the price of the core product, while the downsell should be closer to 1.5-2x more than the core product, and should only be offered after your customer rejects the initial upsell/cross-sell offer. If you are offering your complete library in hardcover for $500, a downsell might see you offering either a portion of your library or your complete library in ebook for $100-$150.

A *bump offer* is a small checkbox that appears on the checkout page that allows for a "one-time purchase" with a single button click. They happen before the first purchase, and can either be an upsell or a cross-sell.

When you're looking for a direct sales solution, whatever you choose should have this functionality, Whether it's Thrivecart, Shopify, WooCommerce, Optimize Press, or whatever you choose to use, this functionality is critical because these offers are almost all profit.

That's why they are Profit Maximizers. Ideally, 20% of your customers would take the bump offer, and another 20% would take your cross-sell/upsell/downsell offer.

If you can make these numbers work, you are bringing significant additional revenue into your business, and this revenue should be almost all profit.

TOFU – TOP OF FUNNEL

Which ecosystem is the best at this part? Deserts.

Deserts are amazing at finding **arbitrage** between reader demand and book supply, and presenting enticing offers to potential readers.

Arbitrage is about discovering opportunities where demand outstrips supply, and using that difference to generate interest from potential readers to get them to take action on your offer before that gap evaporates.

In a way, Deserts are also dealing with excitement, but instead of baking that into an irresistible offer, they are trying to skim the "easy" sale by offering something that a hungry audience already wants.

This allows their offers to be quite a bit more basic than that of a Tundra because they are looking to capitalize on a market while demand is high and supply is low. When the arbitrage dries up in a market a Desert usually moves on because their offer is not complex enough, or expensive enough, to compete in a more competitive environment.

However, because a Desert is great at getting people into funnels, they are naturals at creating TOFU offers, which are the low-cost tripwire and free opt-in offers we give people to find

If a Desert chooses to stay inside a particular market instead of jumping around, they can quickly become experts at creating new **opt-in offers** and putting them in front of potential customers consistently.

Every time the market gets cold, a Desert can switch up their offer and create arbitrage almost at will.

Not only is a Desert great at TOFU, but they actively enjoy fiddling with different types of offers and trying to find ways to get new people into their funnels. I'm not just talking about offering free books, either. You can offer cheat sheets, social calendars, maps, side stories, character art, or just about anything to entice people to enter a funnel, but the key to TOFU is in getting somebody to opt-in to a small offer in order to whet their appetite for buying your BOFU offer.

For example, I have dozens of ebooks, cheat sheets, and other things I can offer at any time to get people interested in both my fiction and non-fiction businesses. Each one is targeted at a different segment of people interested in my

BOFU offers. The more of these you have, the more ins you have with your potential customers to get them to enter your funnel.

The reason we talked about this directly after the BOFU is that these TOFU offers have to attract the right kind of person for your BOFU offer, otherwise, they won't work to convert potential readers into buyers.

TOFU is very different from the "attract" stage of the flywheel we will discuss below. While it's possible to combine the two and have extensive overlap, for our purposes that phase is all about content marketing and SEO and TOFU is about presenting simple opt-in offers meant to hook new customers quickly and bring them into the sales process.

MOFU – MIDDLE OF FUNNEL

Which ecosystem is the best at this part? Depends.

We're going to talk a lot more about MOFU below because a lot of MOFU involves creating a great flywheel. Everyone both inside and outside of your sales funnel will eventually end up in your flywheel, but the most important part of MOFU is to optimize conversions for your BOFU offer. This includes webinars, automation sequences, communities, and more.

While your flywheel can ***also*** deliver this value, you should think of every piece of MOFU content as a way to break down barriers to help customers see the value of your BOFU offer. The main delivery mechanism for your MOFU will probably be an autoresponder that indoctrinates people into your ecosystem and tells customers about the benefits of your BOFU.

An autoresponder, or indoctrination sequence, is an automated series of emails your subscribers start receiving after they sign up for your email list. These emails are staggered throughout several days or weeks so that people unfamiliar with your brand learn who you are and what you do.

With every email, you break through one of the objections holding people back from buying and help them build a deeper connection with you. While a flywheel can have focus as well, MOFU content should be laser-focused on helping to sell your BOFU offer.

Ideally, you would deliver MOFU content in something akin to a sideways sales letter for each of your major series.

You are basically showing off your series over the course of several different emails that rely on different psychological triggers to get people excited to read it. Every autoresponder will be different but for a series BOFU offer, here is what a very simple sequence might look like:

- **Email 1:** Enthusiastic introduction to the series
- **Email 2:** What's different about this series?
- **Email 3:** The main character(s)
- **Email 4:** The main conflict
- **Email 5:** The world
- **Email 6:** Reviews and praise
- **Email 7:** Why you should buy now

Meanwhile, you are running an evergreen countdown timer on your site to help entice readers to buy now before time runs out. Evergreen timers allow you to present a new offer with its own time-limit for each person that hits your page.

You should have a different autoresponder for each core product you're launching and they should rely heavily on these psychological triggers. This differs significantly from the flywheel, which is about consistently delivering value to your audience that **attracts**, **engages**, and **delights** them.

WHAT IS A FLYWHEEL?

Now that we've talked about how to funnel people into your business, we need to create a Flywheel so our efforts grow exponentially while our efforts either stay the same or decrease.

The goal of a flywheel is to **attract** new customers, **engage** them, and then **delight** them with your work in a cyclical manner that centers the customer experience. By creating this flywheel for your business, you are able to build your network and audience with the least amount of effort and minimal downside.

The reason people like this model over the funnel is because it centers the customer experience, and retention, above revenue. If you remember us talking about the sales funnel, **Retention** and **Advocacy** were huge parts of any successful business, and the flywheel is a wonderful mechanic to foster that part of your ecosystem.

Additionally, it can be very helpful for the MOFU activities we talked about above, as potential customers enter your flywheel before they buy and use what they learn inside of it to make purchasing decisions. Additionally, a properly functioning flywheel can also help your TOFU activities by helping you attract more potential customers.

Because of this, the flywheel sits in superposition, both inside your funnel and under it. In a well-functioning business, the sales funnel and flywheel reinforce each other.

ATTRACT

Which ecosystem is the best at this part? Grasslands

In short, TOFU deals with a focused **call to action**, whether through advertising or organic reach, while the attract stage is about the long-term cycle of creating content to draw in your audience.

While good content marketing often has a call to action, they are considerably subtler than the way we think about TOFU marketing.

That is why we say the attract stage is the strength of a Grassland, who is most comfortable writing and producing **at least weekly content** over a long time horizon (1-2 years+) about the same topic until they rank highly in their given topic and can continue to reap the benefits of that thought leadership for years to come.

This is why a Grassland can be subtler with their calls to action. They are relying on the thought leadership advantage that comes from people seeking them out and wanting to work with them.

Even when it comes to social media content, the way we think about attracting new readers is by simply being a constant presence in their lives while the way we think about TOFU activities is by presenting them with a new book or an offer to bring them into a funnel.

These are both crucial activities, but one takes advantage of the short-term arbitrage of the offer (which is the purview of the Desert) while the other takes advantage of the long-term depth of knowledge of a Grassland.

ENGAGE

Which ecosystem is the best at this part? Forests.

The "engage" phase is about being present for your potential customers and showing them the value of your community, which is why it's the advantage of the Forest, who are all about interconnectivity, shared language, and making readers feel like they are part of their "in-crowd".

This doesn't mean you have to have a 100,000-person subreddit like Brandon Sanderson. We talk to Forests all the time who don't want to have a Facebook group or any sort of formal community, but their readers still seem to find each other anyway. This is because they build community into their books through in-jokes and shared language. This shared language bonds people together even if you don't formalize that bond with a reader community.

Even if you don't have a formal community, you will certainly have at least a newsletter where you can engage with readers and show them why they should become a member of your community. Forests often love to offer engagement questions in their newsletters to keep up with their readers, and we think they should lean into that instinct. These questions could be anything from "What did you do this weekend?" to "What is your favorite book?" to anything you can imagine.

The key to this phase of the flywheel is for readers to develop a relationship with you that feels like you care about the same things they care about, and that you understand their pain points.

While during the attract phase you are signaling that you understand the general pain points a reader goes through, the engage phase is really about personalizing that understanding so your readers feel cared for and understood.

This does **not** mean reaching out to them all individually, but instead making them believe that you are there to care for them if they ever need you. *Just make sure to set boundaries.* Forests are particularly bad at giving more of themselves then they can energetically afford to lose. *One key to a good community is that they can exist and connect without you even being there.*

DELIGHT

Which ecosystem is the best at this part? Aquatics.

The final stage of the flywheel *(although it's a circle so it never really ends, just loops back around on itself)* is the delight stage. The delight stage is all about providing unique and overwhelmingly positive experiences to your readers that they will remember and carry with them.

Just like how the attract stage can be partially mapped onto the TOFU, the delight stage can be partially mapped onto the BOFU. After all, a major way to delight your audience is with products they will love.

However, that is not the only way, which is where the delight stage differs from BOFU. In a sales funnel, all that matters is the offer and the sale. There are millions of ways to delight an audience that moves beyond what you are selling them, and delighting audiences with different formats and experiences is where Aquatics excel.

Aquatics think of themselves as "brand managers" for their universes, and that extends to how they think about their fandom. If they can find ways to bring people further into their world, they are going to take it.

This ability to delight is why I believe Aquatics have the highest superfan ratio of any ecosystem. They easily move beyond satisfaction to delight readers by sending them Christmas cards, reading their books on YouTube, creating a fan experience with them like riding horseback together, or any number of ways that make them unforgettable to their readers.

Aquatics are always thinking past the current offer into how they can deliver even more value to their readers. They are the grandmother who is always in the middle of cooking an amazing meal to make sure you leave more than satisfied. We all remember that special food that feels like home, and that feeling is the special purview of the Aquatic.

BRINGING IT ALL TOGETHER

Now that we've talked about each section of this system, how do we bring it all together?

First, we have to find out where you are strong and weak. To start, take out a piece of paper and rate yourself on how much time you spend on your TOFU, MOFU, BOFU, Attract, Engage, and Delight activities on a scale from 1-10.

Then, rank them by how much time you spend on each activity. Finally, rate yourself on how successful you are at each activity.

Here's the twist. *You can't use 7.* Why? Because that is the default number everyone uses when they don't want to commit. You have to either choose between 1-6 or 8-10.

A quick tip: You shouldn't rate yourself a 9 or a 10 unless you are killing it in that activity. Unless you're getting serious ROI on any single activity, you are at best an 8. I'm a pretty successful creator and the only thing I would rate myself a 10 in is BOFU activities. I survive because I create world-class offers. I'm probably a 9 at the attract stage and MOFU, a 6 at TOFU and the delight stage, and a 5 at the engage stage.

That is painful to look at, but based on conversations with Monica and my mastermind, I think that's brutally accurate.

Notice that I'm a Tundra and I'm strongest at the activity that best maps to my strengths. Your rankings should similarly match up pretty well with your base ecosystem, but they might not…and if not that's a problem.

Lots of Forests, for instance, are working hard on TOFU activities, which takes away from where they should be focusing, bumping up their engagement activities because that's where their natural tendencies lie and they'll have the most effortless success.

Now, it's time to get in alignment. Focus on getting one activity up to a 9 or 10, and then move yourself around either the flywheel or funnel to buttress everything else.

If that doesn't resonate with you, or you want results fast, then the one thing that will give you the biggest ROI the quickest is to focus on BOFU offers. Really, everything in your business centers around the offers you make, and if you're not good at designing and stacking offers, the single best thing you can do is get really good at doing that.

FINAL THOUGHTS

There are no more important concepts to your business than the flywheel and the funnel. However, individually they are far from perfect.

The funnel model functions as a way to bring people through a sales process, but once they buy (or don't) customers are then dumped summarily into a vacuum of nothingness as if they have no value. However, the true value of a fan is more than just a $20 bill.

They are human, after all, and humans have value for simply existing. It feels really crappy to simply abandon them on a personal level.

It's also bad business. A major component of business growth comes from selling repeat customers new products and services, not solely through finding new business, making a sales funnel suboptimal for continued growth.

Centering the customer experience is something the flywheel does really well. However, the flywheel is a bit sloppy and haphazard. There's very little direction about when or how somebody enters your flywheel, or how to turn their excitement into revenue, which is where the sales funnel shines.

We believe it is ideal to blend the two. I use sales funnels as a way to bring people into my universe, but once customers finish a funnel, they enter my flywheel, which centers the customer experience for the rest of their time with me, until the next sales event.

Conversely, if they enter my flywheel first, there are several ways for them to enter funnels to learn more about specific products. I like to consider all of my funnels to be little more than spokes in my promotional wheel, leading out from my flywheel.

I love how these two mechanics can blend seamlessly together to create a strong customer experience.

I am trying to build ways for people to enter my ecosystem, and then keep them inside my flywheel for the long haul. None of my sales funnels or platforms are the center of my flywheel. They are just onramps. If an onramp breaks, the flywheel keeps functioning.

CHAPTER 13

WRITING IN YOUR AUTHOR ECOSYSTEM

Writing has always been a deeply personal journey, yet for decades, authors have been squeezed into narrowly defined boxes of genre, style, and approach. Traditional publishing wisdom suggested a one-size-fits-all model of storytelling. You learn the rules, then follow the formula, and success will follow. But what if the key to unlocking your true writing potential lies not in conforming to external expectations, but in understanding your own unique Author Ecosystem?

Just as natural ecosystems in the world have distinct characteristics, each with its own balance, rhythm, and method of survival, so too do writers have inherent creative landscapes that shape how they approach storytelling.

Writers approach stories differently. While one writer might craft a narrative that precisely hits market trends, writing quickly and strategically, another would weave a deeply personal narrative, infusing the story with their unique perspective and creating a world that feels intimately connected to their own experiences. Neither approach is inherently superior. They are simply different expressions of creative energy.

That is the heart of the Author Ecosystems. It gives context to different ways to have success as an author.

This chapter explores how different Author Ecosystems manifest in both fiction and non-fiction writing. We'll journey through five distinct authorial landscapes: the trend-riding Desert, the depth-exploring Grassland, the excitement-generating Tundra, the personality-driven Forest, and the universe-building Aquatic. Each Ecosystem offers a unique lens through which stories are conceived, developed, and brought to life.

More than a writing guide, this exploration is an invitation to recognize and celebrate your natural creative tendencies. By understanding your Ecosystem, you can stop fighting against your inherent writing style and instead learn to harness its unique strengths.

THE DESERT

Deserts are the literary world's most adaptable ecosystem. Like the resilient plants that thrive in arid landscapes, they don't fight the environment. They become masters of it. Their writing isn't about personal expression as much as it is about connection, about understanding the invisible currents of reader desire that flow beneath the surface of the literary marketplace.

Take romance novels, for instance. While some writers might spend months crafting a love story based purely on their personal vision, a Desert writer walks a more strategic path. They're not just telling a story. They're engaging in a sophisticated dialogue with readers' deepest current yearnings. When workplace romances start trending, they don't just notice. They understand why, and how to deliver a perfect experience for fans of that subgenre. Is it a reflection of changing professional dynamics? A desire for narratives of mutual respect? The Desert writer doesn't just observe these shifts; they translate them into narrative.

This doesn't make their work less creative. It requires the ability to be simultaneously responsive and original. It's like being a jazz musician who can improvise brilliantly within a specific musical framework, rather than a classical performer strictly following every note of the sheet music.

In non-fiction, this approach becomes even more pronounced. During the early months of the COVID-19 pandemic, Desert writers were the first to produce practical guides about remote work, mental health resilience, and navigating unprecedented personal challenges. They didn't wait for perfect information. They responded to an immediate need, providing clarity when readers were most hungry for understanding.

But this approach isn't without its challenges. The Desert ecosystem demands constant vigilance. It requires writers to be part storyteller, part cultural anthropologist who are always scanning, always listening. The risk is becoming so focused on trends that you lose the core of storytelling: genuine human connection.

The most successful Desert writers understand this delicate balance. They're not trend-chasers, but trend-interpreters. They don't just follow the market. They help shape it, offering narratives that feel simultaneously familiar and fresh.

The Desert ecosystem isn't about sacrificing art for commerce. It's about recognizing that true art often lies in creating stories that speak directly to the moment, which help readers make sense of their rapidly changing world.

In the vast, shifting landscape of storytelling, Desert writers are the ultimate navigators. They don't fight the terrain. They become one with it.

THE GRASSLAND

Grassland writers are the deep-root systems of the literary world. While other ecosystems might chase the quick bloom of trends or the flashy surface of storytelling, Grasslands are busy building entire worlds of understanding that can sustain readers for generations.

In fiction, this means creating universes so rich and comprehensive that readers don't just enter a story. They inhabit an entire ecosystem of imagination. George R.R. Martin didn't just write a fantasy series; he constructed a world so intricate that fans could spend decades exploring its history, linguistics, and cultural nuances. Each book becomes not just a narrative, but a gateway to a deeper, more complex understanding of human nature.

Non-fiction Grassland writers approach their subjects with similar depth. They aren't content with surface-level explanations or quick takes. When Yuval Noah Harari writes about human history, he's not simply recounting events. He's weaving a comprehensive understanding that connects seemingly disparate threads of human experience, showing how our past shapes our present and future.

This approach requires a kind of intellectual courage that goes beyond typical storytelling. Grassland writers must be willing to spend years developing a single concept. They understand that true expertise isn't about knowing everything quickly, but about knowing something so thoroughly that its complexity becomes beautiful.

Their writing process is less about productivity and more about exploration. Where a Desert writer might produce multiple books in a year, a Grassland writer might spend years on a single project, turning each idea like a gemstone, examining it from every possible angle. It's not inefficiency; it's commitment.

This doesn't mean Grassland writers are slow or academic. Their work pulses with life precisely because of its depth. They're not detached observers, but passionate investigators who bring entire worlds to life through meticulous research and profound insight.

In science fiction, this might mean creating technological systems so believable that they feel like blueprints for future innovation. In historical writing, it means reconstructing past worlds with such vivid detail that readers can smell the air, hear the conversations, understand the hidden motivations behind historical moments.

The greatest risk for a Grassland writer is getting lost in the details, becoming so fascinated by the complexity of their subject that they lose the narrative thread. The most successful Grasslands learn to balance depth with accessibility, creating work that is simultaneously scholarly and deeply engaging.

Sarah understood this. Her books weren't just stories or research. They were invitations asking readers to dig deeper, to see the world not as a collection of isolated facts, but as a complex, interconnected system waiting to be understood.

In a world that often celebrates speed and surface-level understanding, Grassland writers remind us that some stories require patience. Some truths can only be revealed through careful, persistent cultivation. They don't just write books. They grow entire worlds.

THE TUNDRA

Tundra writers are the performance artists of the literary world. Where other writers might see a book as a static object, Tundras see a living, breathing experience carefully orchestrated for maximum impact. Their writing isn't just about telling a story; it's about generating a wave of excitement that sweeps readers into an immersive narrative journey.

At the heart of the Tundra approach lies a masterful understanding of what makes stories compelling. These writers don't just use tropes. They stack them with surgical precision, creating narratives that hit multiple reader pleasure points simultaneously. Imagine a fantasy novel that combines the Chosen One narrative, a complex magic system, and a found family arc. Each element is carefully selected not just for its individual appeal, but for how it interacts with the others, creating a narrative ecosystem more exciting than any single element could be.

This approach requires a deep, almost instinctual understanding of storytelling mechanics. Tundra writers are like literary DJs, mixing familiar beats in ways that feel both nostalgic and completely fresh. They know that readers don't want entirely new experiences. They want exciting reimaginings of stories they already love.

In non-fiction, this translates to books that feel like transformative events. A Tundra self-help author doesn't just offer advice. They create a narrative of personal revolution. They stack motivational techniques, personal anecdotes, and actionable strategies in a way that makes readers feel they're on the cusp of a life-changing moment.

The launch becomes as important as the book itself. Where other writers might see a book release as a simple transaction, Tundras see it as a carefully choreographed performance. They understand that excitement is a renewable resource. If managed correctly, each launch can feed into the next, creating a cycle of anticipation and satisfaction.

This doesn't mean their work is shallow. Far from it. The most successful Tundra writers understand that true excitement comes from depth carefully packaged in an accessible form. They're not afraid to tackle complex ideas, but they do so with a sense of narrative momentum that keeps readers turning pages.

The greatest challenge for Tundra writers is maintaining momentum. Their natural cycle is one of intense activity followed by periods of recovery. The most successful learn to use this rhythm, creating launches that feel like literary festivals, followed by thoughtful periods of reflection and preparation.

In a publishing world that often feels dominated by careful calculation or pure artistic expression, Tundra writers remind us that storytelling is also about joy, about the pure excitement of a narrative that makes your heart race and your imagination soar. They don't just write books. They create experiences that make readers feel alive.

THE FOREST

Writing begins as an act of vulnerability for Forest authors. It's not about telling a story so much as revealing a piece of oneself, creating a landscape where readers don't just visit, but become permanent residents of a deeply personal world.

Their worlds are constructed not from external research or market trends, but from the rich internal terrain of personal experience. Their writing transcends genre. A Forest author might write a murder mystery, a sweet romance, and a speculative fiction novel that all feel fundamentally different yet unmistakably connected by a singular voice.

This isn't about narcissism. It's about authenticity. A Forest writer's superpower lies in their ability to inject their unique perspective into every narrative, creating a shared language that transforms readers from passive consumers into active participants in a collaborative storytelling experience.

In fiction, this means creating characters that feel less like fictional constructs and more like extensions of the author's own complex inner world. These characters don't just move through a plot. They embody different facets of human experience, filtered through the author's distinctive lens of understanding. When a reader says, "This feels like something only [Author] could have written," they're acknowledging the Forest writer's true gift.

Non-fiction becomes equally personal. A Forest writer doesn't simply present information. They weave personal narrative, research, and insight into a tapestry that feels both deeply informative and intimately human. Their books become conversations, inviting readers to see the world from a unique perspective rather than presenting a detached, objective view.

The greatest challenge for Forest writers is finding balance. Their natural tendency is to go deep. Sometimes that means going so deep that they risk becoming incomprehensible to readers outside their immediate creative ecosystem. The most successful learn to create entry points, to build bridges that invite readers into their world without overwhelming them.

This approach requires remarkable creative courage. Forest writers must be willing to be vulnerable, to expose the intricate emotional landscapes that drive their storytelling. They create not just books, but entire universes of meaning, inviting readers to see the world through a lens both deeply personal and universally resonant.

Their writing becomes a bridge between individual experience and collective understanding. Where other ecosystems might see writing as a product or a trend, Forest writers see it as a living, breathing entity, constantly evolving, constantly revealing new layers of human complexity. They don't just write books. They create worlds where readers can discover new ways of understanding themselves.

THE AQUATIC

Imagine storytelling not as a linear process of writing a book, but as an expansive ecosystem of narrative experiences. This is the world of the Aquatic writer who sees stories not as static objects, but as living, breathing universes waiting to be explored.

Aquatic writers understand that a story is no longer confined to the printed page. Where other writers see a book as an endpoint, Aquatics see it as a beginning, the first invitation into a much larger experience.

In fiction, this means creating narratives so rich and multidimensional that they naturally expand beyond traditional storytelling formats. Consider how George Lucas didn't just write Star Wars. He created an entire mythology that could be experienced through films, books, comics, games, and countless other media. Each format doesn't just supplement the story; it reveals new dimensions of the universe.

Non-fiction becomes equally immersive. An Aquatic writer doesn't simply share information. They design comprehensive learning experiences. Their books are gateways to entire ecosystems of knowledge, complete with complementary online courses, interactive workshops, community platforms, and multimedia resources that transform passive reading into active engagement.

The core of the Aquatic approach is understanding fan experience. These writers don't just create for an audience. They create *with* them. Every narrative decision considers how fans might interact with the story, how they might expand and explore the universe being constructed. It's a collaborative process where the boundary between creator and audience becomes wonderfully blurred.

This approach requires a remarkable breadth of skills. An Aquatic writer must be part author, part game designer, part brand manager, and part community builder. They need to understand not just storytelling, but user experience, transmedia storytelling, and the intricate dynamics of fan engagement.

The greatest risk for Aquatic writers is spreading themselves too thin, trying to create so many experiences that the core narrative loses its coherence. The most successful learn to create a strong, central vision that can naturally expand into multiple formats without losing its essential character.

This isn't about marketing or commercial strategy, but lies in understanding storytelling as a fundamentally interactive, expansive experience. An Aquatic writer doesn't just tell a story. They create a world that readers can inhabit, explore, and ultimately make their own.

Their books become invitations to step into entire universes of imagination. They don't just write stories. They build worlds that breathe, grow, and transform with every reader's interaction.

FINDING YOUR LITERARY ECOSYSTEM

Writing is not a singular, uniform path, but a vast landscape with multiple terrains, each offering its own unique possibilities for creative expression. There is no universal "right" way to write, only the way that most authentically resonates with your individual creative spirit.

Each Author Ecosystem represents a distinct approach to storytelling, a unique lens through which writers can understand their creative impulses. These aren't rigid categories, but fluid frameworks that help writers recognize their natural strengths and navigate their creative journey.

The Desert writer understands storytelling as a strategic dialogue with reader expectations, crafting narratives that feel simultaneously familiar and fresh. They are the market navigators, able to quickly identify and respond to emerging literary currents. When the wind shifts to a new trend, they will shift, too, content in writing for any audience, as long as they are entertained.

Grassland writers are the deep-root systems of literature, cultivating comprehensive worlds of understanding. Their approach is about depth, patience, and a commitment to exploring complex ideas with meticulous care. They don't just write stories but grow entire ecosystems of knowledge.

Tundra writers are the performance artists of storytelling, understanding that a book is more than a collection of pages. It's an experience. They stack narrative elements with precision, creating works that generate excitement and sweep readers into immersive journeys.

Forest writers transform storytelling into an act of personal revelation. Their strength lies in their ability to inject a unique perspective into every narrative, creating shared languages that invite readers into deeply personal universes of meaning.

Aquatic writers see storytelling as world-building, creating expansive narrative experiences that transcend traditional media. They understand that a story is no longer confined to a book, but can bloom into multiple formats, inviting interactive engagement.

No Author Ecosystem is better or worse than another. Each offers unique strengths and represents a valid approach to creative expression. We know successful authors in every ecosystem. The key is understanding your natural tendencies, embracing them, and learning how to leverage them most effectively.

Successful writers often evolve, incorporating elements from different Ecosystems as they grow. A Desert writer might develop the depth of a Grassland, a Forest writer might learn the strategic approach of a Desert. The boundaries are fluid, the possibilities endless.

Your writing journey is not about fitting into a predetermined mold, but about discovering the creative landscape that allows your voice to flourish most authentically. It's about understanding that your unique way of seeing the world is not a limitation, but your greatest creative asset.

CHAPTER 14

EMAIL MARKETING FOR EVERY AUTHOR ECOSYSTEM

We've all heard the expression "email is king". When it comes to marketing, there is no better investment than building your email list.

If that's true, why do so many authors evade their mailing list like the plague, and why is it so hard for writers to extract value from their email list at a level on par with other industries?

Well, one of the main reasons is that instead of keeping readers in their own direct sales environment to maximize the value of every sale, they are instead sending readers to retailers where they are getting a fractional share of an already minimal average order value.

Most other businesses send subscribers to a web store or sales page with products that range from $20-$1,000+, instead of $1-$10 like on book retailers.

This is the kind of thing The Author Ecosystems can help you with, but that's still only part of the story.

The other part of this story is that every ecosystem should approach email marketing differently based on their strengths and challenges, but we're all told there is only one way to do email marketing.

You should know by now that there is not a one-size-fits-all strategy to anything, especially email. In this article, I'm going to break down an email strategy for each ecosystem that will hopefully make you fall in love with email marketing.

DESERT

Advantages: Because of their desire to optimize every part of their business, it's easy to see why the traditional email strategy pushed by the publishing industry won't work for a Desert. It's a ton of effort to set up swaps every week, coordinate freebies, and create a gigantic monster of an email that will probably lead to few, if any, sales. *It's a horrible strategy for anyone, but it would be especially frustrating for a Desert.*

Instead, I would recommend Deserts implement something more akin to what Morning Brew, Tim Ferris, or 1440 used to grow their list to 100,000+ without investing a ton of time into any individual newsletter.

Namely, a daily/weekly/monthly digest or roundup where you are gathering the most important news about an industry and disseminating it into short news bites.

This is something Book Riot does already with Today in Books. You can also provide information on an industry, a genre, or just about anything that has a large audience, which is something you are uniquely qualified to analyze.

I also use this strategy with my weekly digests, and it allows me to get an additional email out to subscribers every week with less than an hour of work.

One of the reasons I love this strategy is that it doesn't have to be about you or your books. Deserts usually want to work in the background anyway and let their writing do the talking. This strategy allows you to create a brand around your newsletter that has nothing to do with you while still collecting an audience of fans and funneling them to your work.

The best part of this strategy is that it's almost infinitely scalable with advertising. Companies like Beehiiv and Sparkloop have created recommendation engines like Substack, but they are powered by ads. For instance, Beehiiv has a program called Boosts. Sparkloop has Upscribe and their Partner Network.

What's nice is that you can both make money from the platforms and also spend money to grow with them. I've been testing this out with the Beehiiv network, and while it's more focused on AI and tech than Sparkloop, I've still made $100 in the last week on my recommendations. I plan to dump that money back into ads in order to keep growing.

Challenges: The challenge here is scaling the right audience to buy your books. Hopefully, you're creating an environment where this whole enterprise is profitable by itself, but you should remember that you're looking for people to buy your books at the end of the day…unless you aren't. It's not impossible to build a big email list for a random project, and then sell it through a company like Duuce or Flippa. Then, you can rinse and repeat, or move on to something else.

GRASSLAND

Advantages: While the above strategy can work really well to build up a sizeable email list quickly, Grasslands are more focused on being seen as thought leaders moving the industry forward. A big list is good, but what they're really looking for is influencing the movers and shakers of the industry and causing seismic shifts over a long time horizon.

For this reason, you should consider creating a newsletter that is almost purely value-based and lives on a platform on Substack or your own blog. That way, it has the longevity to keep "putting pennies in the bank" for years.

The main problem with sending a normal promotions email for a Grassland is that you can't disseminate it widely. Once you send it, the value drops to zero, which isn't ideal for a Grassland marketing strategy. Instead, their goal is to make something once and keep extracting value from it forever.

Whereas, if you can create a more content-focused newsletter, it allows you to syndicate it widely and get maximum value out of your work for the longest time.

For instance, this article lives on Substack, but it also gets disseminated over email, and then is cached on Google and other search engines. I could also syndicate it out to Medium and other platforms, though Substack doesn't have that functionality natively.

If I did my job right, then people will be able to search it for years, bringing people into our ecosystem long after it gets emailed out to subscribers.

This is the ideal situation for most Grasslands. A round-up strategy is perfect for Deserts who are trying to tap into the zeitgeist now, but you are more likely trying to tap into where the industry is going in a couple of years.

My main publication offers a new article every week **and** a roundup of my favorite articles from the past week, so I try to have my cake and eat it, too.

One thing you might want to consider to bring in more income is to offer sponsorships like Simon Owens and most mainstream publications do.

You can also use the Paved or Sparkloop network, but you will probably see more success with a deeper partnership you can vet for your audience.

Then, you can put ads in your newsletter or do an advertorial for an advertiser you believe in to share with your audience.

You are probably already covering the industry closely, so it would make sense for advertisers to work with you. If you have a stellar reputation you can probably charge top dollar for a spot in your publication.

The advantage of an advertising strategy is that when you have something to promote, you can pop it inside the ad spot and use it for your own promotion.

If that doesn't work for you, then you can offer a membership like Jane Friedman does with the Hot Sheet. Or, you can use it as a launching pad for consulting and courses, like Writers at Work with Sarah Fay or Marlee Grace.

Challenges: Having a value-based newsletter is not the easiest thing to monetize during a launch. Because you are not sending sales emails often, you have not developed the sales habit in your customers. This is why having advertising in your newsletter could be an effective strategy. Not only are you building revenue, but you are also training your subscribers to click and buy.

TUNDRA

Advantages: The hype train is strong with you, so you're going to get a lot of value out of building up an audience and then monetizing them with launch events.

It's best to think of your email strategy in three stages: ***Building, Launching, and Recovery.*** I try to think of my release calendar in seasons, with every launch being the crescendo of the wave I'm building up to or recovering from. Knowing that, I set my launches based on when I know I can crescendo effectively.

There are three parts to a launch: Prep, Launch, and Recovery. In prep, I build up to my next launch. Then, there is the launch itself. Finally, in recovery, I give both myself and my fans a chance to relax and catch their breath before we do it again.

For me, that means January, March, June, and September, I launch books. I have always had effective launches in those months for different reasons.

In January and June, there are fewer books launching, so I can capitalize on that with my less popular books. In March and September, there are tons of books launching, so I put out my most popular books then so they get the most eyeballs on them.

Once that is set, I know I need to spend a month building up to that launch, which means the lowest point on the release wave will occur every year in December, February, May, and August… My biggest book launches last 31 days, and my shortest can be as short as five days. It all depends on the project and how much I think people can stand me talking about it.

It's important to note that this is my launch schedule for core books ONLY. I lay this out FIRST, before anything else, including experimental projects and other things I'm adding to the mix.

Then, I plan every other launch around this schedule, as it is my moneymaker. It took me a LONG time to learn this, and it wasn't until I did that I had any consistency in my career.

Once I have planned these core launches, I figure out what else I want to try in the remaining time.

This brings us to the next thing. ***In the building phase,*** you're using places like Bookfunnel, StoryOrigin, Bookdoggy, Booksweeps, and Written Word Media to build up a big mailing list, along with organic traffic and advertising. The goal here is really to give value with a free book or other piece of content. Then, use an automated email sequence to get them excited about your work.

An email sequence is a series of marketing messages targeting your audience on a set schedule.

If you already use email sequence software, you know there are several types of automation that can be used to reach your audience. With email sequencing, you use marketing automation software to set up and publish these campaigns depending on the actions they've taken on your website.

Email sequences are also known as lifecycle emails and email marketing automation because they allow you to schedule specific content to be sent out.

These new emails should be segmented out from your main list so they don't get your main emails. However, that doesn't mean that your main list doesn't get love during the building phase, too.

During this phase, you are delivering value weekly by sharing free books, behind-the-scenes processes, and generally getting people to know you, like you, and trust you. More importantly, you are using this time to get them excited for your next big project.

It's really important that you focus on sending emails with *one* call-to-action, or "thing you want somebody to do".

Ideally, you want them to do one thing with every email. The emails you write in any of these phases, but especially this one, should be short and fun.

Our goal is to crescendo our building phase to maximize excitement at the launch of our next product or project. The whole of our marketing should be about cresting and receding like waves so that we can maximize our launches. I call this ***a rolling launch strategy*** because they rise and fall a bit like a series of rolling hills or rolling waves.

During the launch phase, you'll be sending way more launch emails than any of the other ecosystems. I recommend daily emails during a launch, each one highlighting a different part of your exciting new project.

Here is a sample email strategy during a launch, from *Get Your Book Selling on Kickstarter*.

- **Day 1 (Tuesday) - 3 emails -** I send a "we launched" email in the morning with a graphic of my early bird perks. Then, I send a mid-morning bonus perk email assuming we do well enough to qualify for it. Often, this perk is tied to backing on the first day only. Then, I send a final email at night saying the first-day "bonus" perk is going away.
- **Day 2 (Wednesday) - 1 email -** The first day is for hitting people that already know and love the book. The second day is about introducing people to the book a second time, sending the blurb and going into depth about the book.
- **Day 3 (Thursday) - 1 email -** This email is to tell people there are only two days left for early bird perks. I use this email to talk about early bird perks. I recommend having 4-5 early bird perks available for backers
- **Day 4 (Friday) - 1 email -** This one is to say there is only 1 day left for early bird perks.

- **Day 5 (Saturday) - 2 emails -** I send a "last day for early bird perks" in the morning. Then, a "last chance for early bird perks" at night. I have tested this all sorts of different ways, and sending the second email is very effective.
- **Day 6 (Sunday) - 0 emails -** break.
- **Day 7 (Monday) - 1 email -** This is an email talking about week 2 perks. I recommend 4-5 week two perks. This also sets up that you'll be spending the second week going deep on different aspects of the book.
- **Day 8 (Tuesday) - 1 email -** Dive deeper into the main character or the story idea (though you probably covered the story in the previous week's emails.
- **Day 9 (Wednesday) - 1 email -** Dive deeper into the setting, or the art, or another part of the book.
- **Day 10 (Thursday) - 1 email -** Dive deeper into the reason you made the book. This is your WHY email, and critically important to get people who've heard all about the book and just need one little push to go over the edge.
- **Day 11 (Friday) - 1 email -** 1 day left for week 2 perks. This is the same as the previous week.
- **Day 12 (Saturday) - 2 emails -** Last day for week 2 perks in the morning. Then, last chance for week 2 perks at night. These emails are exactly like the first week's emails.
- **Day 13 (Sunday) - 0 emails -** break.
- **Day 14 (Monday) - 1 email -** Introducing final week perks. You don't have to go as hard this week. You can just have 2-3 perks for this, since you'll get a lot of traction out of the campaign ending.

- **Day 15 (Tuesday) - 1 email -** I send a "2 days left" email in the morning, knowing that Kickstarter sends a "48 hours left" email to people watching the campaign in the afternoon.
- **Day 16 (Wednesday) - 2 emails -** 1 day left in the morning. 24 hours left in the afternoon, or whenever there are only 24 left in the campaign.
- **Day 17 (Thursday) - 4 emails -** 12 hours left, 8 hours left, 4 hours left, 2 hours left.

This can get very exhausting, which is why we need so much recovery time after a launch, for both ourselves and our audiences to settle from the excitement and reset.

Challenges: The challenge of a Tundra is they always want to launch the next thing, and they don't take into account the building or recovery phase. If you don't have ways to build up your audience between launches, then you will see your success dwindle.

You also have to contend with the fact that launch emails lose all value the minute after you send them.

Most importantly, if you're not delivering a ton of value to your audience between launches, they will think you are just withdrawing from the goodwill bank instead of making deposits into it.

Think about your goodwill like it's a bank. We'll call it The First Bank of Goodwill. This bank works like any other bank, except that it runs on your goodwill instead of money.

When you do something nice for somebody, you make a deposit into this bank. Whether it's writing a blog post, speaking on a panel, providing advice over coffee, or even just retweeting an interesting article, everything you do for your audience is a deposit in the goodwill bank.

By contrast, everything you ask of your audience is a withdrawal from the goodwill bank. Every time you ask somebody to buy your product, every time you pitch them something, and every single time you ask them to share your posts, you are withdrawing from your goodwill account.

If you have been depositing into the goodwill bank over and over again, you can make these withdrawals without overdrafting your account; however, if you haven't been making these deposits, then you can't afford to make an ask of your audience. Imagine trying to buy a $50,000 boat in cash when your checking account only has $3.27 in it. You can't do that.

The same is true with your goodwill.

You absolutely must focus equally on all three phases to make the most out of this strategy. Unlike some other ecosystems that can supplement their income with advertising, you probably don't need that kind of stuff because you're constantly in a launch cycle.

FOREST

Advantages: The people who designed the email strategy people teach for the publishing industry must be Forests because the only ecosystem that could get away with the type of email we're told to make are Forests, who have very, very forgiving audiences.

Additionally, the only people who would possibly spend the hours upon hours it takes to design one of those emails are Forests, who will spend countless hours making something if they think their audience will like it, even if they don't sleep for a week.

I think a lot about RJ Blain and her Sneaky Kitty Critic email list "written by her cats". Even after knowing her for years, I have no idea what she's doing with her email. ***It's chaotic, but I love it.*** She knows how to engage her perfect people and make them feel special.

That's what really matters. Forests know their audience so well they can send just about anything and their audience will eat it up.

Because Forests have such devoted audiences, they are also the only ones who should be even thinking about monthly emails over weekly ones, and only then because they probably have a Circle community, a Facebook group, a Discord channel, or somewhere else where they interact with their readers all the time. If you have that kind of interaction with people, you don't need to send them a lot of emails.

Even if you send monthly emails, you might also want to consider doing a weekly digest of comments from your group, or something similar.

This is something you can set up automatically on some services, but you might have to do it by hand, or have an assistant do it.

Kathryn Vercillo does these amazing roundup of interactions she's had/seen in the past week which I think could be really interesting for a Forest to explore.

Challenges: Forests are incredible at making their own people feel special, but an email list is also a great way to find new people. Everything I mentioned above is great fan service, but you also have to develop a good autoresponder to bring people into your ecosystem and make sure they are set up for success.

Don't assume everyone on your list knows what you're talking about, especially if they are new. I suggest you segment out new people and run them through an extensive email sequence to make sure they are well-educated on your space before you show them maximum weirdness.

The key to a Forest succeeding with email is consistency. If they can develop consistently, then they can send just about anything to their audience.

AQUATIC

Advantages: Aquatics are almost the perfect marketing chameleon who can get a lot of value from integrating anything I've talked about so far into their email practice.

Because they are building one overriding fan experience across many formats, they can create a huge audience through advertising and digests or create unique fan experiences like a Forest. They will probably be launching often, so having a rolling promotion strategy of a Tundra would work for them, too.

The question for an Aquatic is where to start, and that's kind of always their problem with just about anything. They want to do everything all the time and are most prone to shiny object syndrome.

The key for an Aquatic is to figure out which strategy to try first and that's going to depend on where you are in your career.

If you are "pre-launch", you probably want to start building up an audience either like a Desert or like a Tundra, depending on which strategy feels right to you. The further you are away from launch, the more you should probably build like a Desert.

Why not a Grassland? Because nobody knows your universe yet, and so you'll get the most value at building a "look-alike" audience filled with a ton of people you think would like your universe, but since there's nothing out about it yet, you also have no hype. Instead, you could build on the hype other universes already have going for them while you build up your own.

Once you have an audience, keeping them engaged like a Forest makes a lot of sense. I would probably say that the last thing you should build is your Grassland-ed-ness, which seems to go against the true power of a Grassland, but people aren't going to be interested in doing a deep dive into your universe until after you have a fandom, and you'll probably get the least from content marketing than a

Grassland because your universe will likely be quite niche for a long while.

Challenges: An Aquatic's biggest challenge is F.O.C.U.S. They have a ton of trouble focusing on one challenge until they have success with it. They have big plans and huge ambitions. Because they have a thousand options of what to do next, they end up flitting between them, which is a really bad way to have success. You can have success in any one of these areas, but you have to pick one and stick with it until you either break through or you're sure it won't work for you.

By the way, it's fine to give up on something. Just know why you're doing it and make sure it's a good reason. Don't just give up because another pretty thing came up that you're dying to try.

FINAL THOUGHTS

Email marketing isn't easy, especially when you're first getting started, but it's considerably easier once you have a process in place that works for you. Like any good flywheel, it gets easier the more you do it.

For years when I was getting started, I did something called **7 Cool Things**, which was modeled on *Tim Ferris's Five Bullet Friday*. It was easy. It was fun. It gave my audience something of me when I didn't have anything to talk about with my own work.

Then, I started to launch more often and fell into the rhythm of build, launch, recover. In the past year, I've focused heavily on Substack and building like a Grassland.

There is no wrong answer, and if you see a strategy above that resonates with you outside of your ecosystem, try it.

The biggest thing that determines a successful email strategy is consistency. That said, the goal of each strategy I've outlined above is different. ***Only the Tundra is really set up to maximize money from the launch itself***, which is why I showed other ecosystems different ways to generate income that might work better depending on your ecosystem.

The goal of email is often less about making money from a launch than keeping yourself at the top of people's minds so that when you're ready to launch they can find your work and make space for it.

At The Author Stack, we have a Grassland strategy on Substack while having a Tundra strategy on Convertkit. We have both a promotions email list and a value-based email list, and each has a different purpose. One helps us continuously grow, while the other helps us monetize to stay in business.

CHAPTER 15

WEBSITE SALES FOR EVERY AUTHOR ECOSYSTEM

Website sales are as simple as they are complicated. Webstores, for instance, are the thing most associated with direct sales in the author community. Anyone who has read our work or heard us talk knows that's utter nonsense, but Shopify specifically has done a great job convincing people that if you have a webstore then you are doing direct sales, and otherwise you're not doing it at all, even if you run Kickstarters, manage a successful Ream/Patreon/Substack, and attend conventions.

Interestingly enough, webstores aren't even the only type of direct sales you can have on your website. You can host landing pages on your website without ever having a webstore. I have seen people run crowdfunding campaigns and subscriptions on their websites. I have even seen people host virtual conventions there as well.

For our purposes, though, we're going to be talking about the two main types of website sales; webstores and landing pages.

Webstores are web pages where you list your work for sale in a catalog, like Amazon, but with direct access to your readers.

While services like Shopify, Payhip, Gumroad,
and Woocommerce are most often associated with
webstore sales, we also consider sites like Etsy to be
webstore sales. Even though an Etsy store doesn't exactly
exist on your website, the functionality of how you set one
up and the methodology about how you succeed is similar
enough that we're squeezing them together. Additionally, a
site like Teachable that lists multiple courses would also be
considered a webstore.

As long as you have direct access to the customer, then we
consider it direct sales. If, however, you sell on a site that
doesn't give you direct access to your customers, then we
would consider that retailer or catalog sales. Still good, just
a different thing.

Landing pages, by contrast, don't usually list multiple
products, but present one compelling offer to customers for
a single product. A landing page might look like
a Bookfunnel page asking you to opt-in to join your
mailing list. You could also set one up
on Clickfunnel or OptimizePress to sell a product.

A landing page could be set up to run consistently, or it
could be a special offer only available for a limited time.
Just like with webstores, you might not set up a landing
page on your own website or you might create a subdomain
that acts like it was built into your webpage while exists
somewhere else entirely.

Personally, I use Payhip for my webstore and
OptimizePress to build most of my landing pages for
Wannabe Press, augmented by Themify and Elementor,
which we used at WriterMBA to create most of our sites.

While my personal website is more complicated than just a single page, our company websites are almost all landing pages set up to drive sales to one of our products.

We'll be talking about both today, as depending on your ecosystem you might have more success with one than the other.

DESERT

Advantages: Deserts are optimization machines, so they will get the most from running cold traffic ads to their webstore and/or landing pages. While they can have success with both, Deserts are probably the only ecosystem that has a reasonable chance of making a profit on a webstore through cold traffic advertising.

Why? Because tedious optimization is their jam and that's the only way to succeed with cold traffic advertising directed at a webstore.

For every other ecosystem, they should focus on running traffic to a landing page (if they run traffic at all), but because Deserts tend to have big backlists and their customers are so used to the retailer experience, they can have success with cold traffic advertising.

Additionally, while we usually recommend authors not try to mimic Amazon and focus their store on selling bundles unavailable on every other site, Deserts should do the opposite and try to mimic the Amazon experience as much as possible, and focus on cross-selling and upselling people into more expensive offers. This is because Deserts are aiming at the middle of the road, quick sale, impulse buy customer, and those readers highly value ease of use.

Because of the complicated nature of what Deserts are setting up, they are also the only ecosystem where using Shopify makes complete sense. Features like browser intent, where you can retarget visitors without anyone signing up, the ability to use ShopPay to streamline the checkout process, and other advanced features make it a no-brainer to spend $100+/mo for all the bells and whistles.

If you are thinking about Shopify, it really only makes sense if you're going to be running advertising traffic to your webstore.

Additionally, we've seen Deserts have great success with optimizing landing pages, specifically for series, especially if they don't have a huge catalog. Deserts are going to be able to pore over the data and make specific and meticulous changes to their site, like changing the color of a button to increase conversions, which most of the other ecosystems aren't going to have the stomach or fortitude to do.

Challenges: Deserts are the most likely to jump on tactics that produce short-term gain. Because they love taking advantage of arbitrage while it exists, they will fall down all sorts of rabbit holes if they are not careful, which could lead their ads to be marked as spam and their tactics frowned upon by advertisers. Even though we don't often see this with Deserts and retailer sales, we have seen it multiple times when Deserts transition their attention to direct sales.

The key to direct sales is consistency over time, and Deserts like to hop from one thing to the next. With direct sales, your goal is to set up something that works for a while, so make sure to chill out a bit. Don't chase every gold rush that comes along even if you can, and try to set up your business for the long term.

GRASSLAND

Advantages: The secret advantage of Grasslands revolves around creating a lot of little hooks back to their work all around the internet, so a smart Grassland will focus on setting up series landing pages and bundles of their work that they can constantly point back to while they're creating content. At the very least, every time you speak or write a post you should have a link to a relevant opt-in that allows you to gather email addresses.

This can be in the form of a cheat sheet, an email course, an ebook, or just about anything designed to get people to your website to sign up. Then, after they sign up, you should have an autoresponder set up to indoctrinate people into your ecosystem and offer them something to buy that is relevant to their interests.

Perhaps somebody signed up to read the first book in your series for free, and now you are giving them a special offer to purchase the rest of the series at a discount, or perhaps you have a cheat sheet on setting up a 401k and you have a landing page offer to do somebody's taxes for 50% off their first year.

Grasslands are experts at providing value and building goodwill, but they need to be better at not only telling people what they do, but offering them something to buy. As for webstores, you'll probably be fine with a Gumroad or Payhip store that doesn't charge a monthly fee since you won't likely be running advertising to it.

It's very important for a Grassland to have all their work available on their website so people can buy when they are ready. I also recommend putting together special bundles with additional content people can't get anywhere else so that it encourages people to buy.

Challenges: Grasslands don't love standing up and saying "Did you know you could buy this?" So, they are very likely to set up the free part of this system and then completely neglect the indoctrination and sales funnel part that tries to extract value from all their hard work. I know Monica and I have been guilty of this, especially while overstressed.

It's great that you keep building those hooks, but we have to turn those hooks into money, which means setting up your landing pages and a webstore so that people know what they can buy. It's very different knowing all about psychological triggers and using them effectively in your business.

TUNDRA

Advantages: Tundras traffic in excitement and there's not a ton exciting about a webstore. So, I think most Tundras, myself included, find them boring. One way I've added some excitement to my webstore is to fill it with exclusives and bundles readers can't get anywhere else.

For instance, I've got about a dozen books available on my webstore that you can only find on my website. So, when readers come to my webstore and see all sorts of new things they can read, they get all sorts of excited.

Additionally, I offer bundles for all my series that include audio commentary and/or AI-read audiobooks that they can't get anywhere else. I'm really trying to delight people with my webstore and give them something unique to convince them to buy from my site instead of a retailer.

I have also set up series landing pages for both my major series that include a one-time offer people can get when they first join my mailing list. While my Godsverse Chronicles is usually $50, I offer it for $20 to new subscribers for the first few days after they join to help encourage people to start reading early.

I also get a lot of value from "special offer" landing pages. Earlier this year I offered a hardcover copy of Ichabod Jones: Monster Hunter volume 1 to people for free if they paid shipping and handling. Then, I offered several upsells which ended up making me good money even giving the first book for free.

These are three ways I've been able to use my website between Kickstarter campaigns to keep the excitement level high and delight readers.

Challenges: All of that is great, but you also need the slow boring work of having things on your webstore and allowing people to buy them. Yes, you need special offers and bundles, but you should also make it easy to buy less expensive things in your store, too, if you want to maximize your money. Even somebody picking up a free book is being taught to buy from your website instead of Amazon.

Tundras want everything to be exciting, which is great, but they shoot themselves in the foot by forcing everything to be these grand spectacles where a lot of selling books is the slow, boring work of adding a few dollars here and there every day of the month and every month of the year.

FOREST

Advantages: Forests love doting on their biggest fans, so the best thing that a Forest can do with their webstore is the exact opposite of what a Desert does with theirs. Deserts are looking to match Amazon as possible, while Forests would benefit from filling their webstore with as much exclusive merch as they can find. Whether it's merch, special editions, merch, or exclusive offers, a Forest webstore should be a way for fans to fall deeper in love with the characters they love.

While I don't think it's a bad idea to have your regular books available on your webstore, they could drown out your exclusive offers, which is where your webstore will shine. If you're using a site like Shopify, then make sure every offer is cross-selling or upselling another piece that will up the cart value on every order and get people to fall deeper in love with you.

While a Desert will want to upsell other books, you will likely get more value on upselling merch or something exclusive that will get your fans to squeal with excitement.

Then, you can augment your webstore with special offer landing pages built around different times of the year or special times inside your universe. If your characters have special holidays or events special to them, use that to make something special for your fans. You could produce a different special offer to your audience as often as every month. I would recommend looking outside books to create packages with other craftspeople that could deepen the experience readers have with your brand.

Challenges: The obvious challenge here is that offering so much exclusive stuff on your webstore could feel isolating to casual fans, but I think that's okay in this case, especially if you provide on-ramps to your work through your special offers and series landing pages. That said, it's definitely something to consider. Could you offer a "featured deal" that is just your full series, or something to hook casual readers?

Or could you just offer a compelling book for free in order to hook those same readers, and then create an automated sequence to bring them through your series and create superfans?

Another thing you could try is a popup that says "New here? Try our newbie sampler for X-percent off," which will help you parse out new people.

While this will be acutely true with new fans, you also run the risk of overwhelming all your diehard fans if you put too many amazing offers on your webstore, which is why you should augment it with your special offers to draw attention to certain things you offer throughout the year.

AQUATIC

Advantages: Since Aquatics love delighting their fans, it's a no-brainer to have tons of merch and extras on your webstore to draw people into your universe. Like a Forest, an Aquatic is trying to get people to fall in love with their universe, but since they're building a trend from the ground up, they also need to be acutely aware that people will often come into your universe without knowing anything about it.

While a Forest should almost exclusively use "deep cuts" from their books on their merch, an Aquatic would likely get a ton of value from making a broader appeal to people who like their genre and using that to start people on a journey to love their brand.

For instance, an Aquatic who writes sci-fi might have a shirt that says "Space Opera lover" that features art from their own universe. People don't need to know their universe to think the shirt is cool, but by exposing them to an Aquatic's world, they help them subconsciously fall in love with their universe.

That's not to say they shouldn't create all sorts of cool pieces from their universe, but an Aquatic would get unique value out of something like creating an RPG of their world built on an existing Dungeons and Dragons system and incorporating other bits of well-known formats that can expose larger audiences to their world and pull them off to fall in love with your universe.

The same is true with landing pages. The more an Aquatic can create broadly appealing offers that feature their universe, exposing people to it through "the side door" as it were, the quicker people will start adopting and noticing your cool universe.

Challenges: The challenge of an Aquatic is that they are creating a trend from scratch, and they want to talk only about their thing, ignoring the fact that most people don't know their universe. They want to talk in code, but nobody knows the code. They need to stay broadly appealing to draw in people from all sorts of modalities while being unique enough to get people excited to stay around. Aquatics have to balance both of these things at the same time, and it's a fine line to walk.

FINAL THOUGHTS

Website sales can be overwhelming, which is why it makes so much sense to break down the components and try to tackle them one step at a time.

- **Webstore exclusives** - Products a buyer can only get, or only get for that price, on your website.
- **Opt-in offers** - Freebie landing pages that bring in new traffic to your email list.
- **Series landing pages** - A landing page offer for each series, or book, you produce. The more books you have in a series, the more compelling the offer.
- **Special offer landing pages** - Special deals and bundles you'll offer once, or once a year, to keep delighting your readers.
- **Mimicking retailers** - Adding your other books that are available from retailers.

I recommend tackling one of these a month, or even one a quarter, before moving on to the next one. Website sales also pair well with crowdfunding. It's quite easy to take your Kickstarter and mold it into a series landing page, then use roughly the same copy to create a webstore exclusive. I've done that several times for my best-selling series.

Additionally, though tedious, it's relatively easy to mimic retailers as you already have all the copy already created from uploading them to those other platforms. All you need to do is copy and paste, for the most part, and then massage it.

For the most part, you can do most of this with a Payhip store and free Elementor plugin for your WordPress site. There are more complex solutions available, but most people can get by, at least at the beginning, with those two largely free elements.

CHAPTER 16

KICKSTARTER FOR EVERY AUTHOR ECOSYSTEM

If you've been following my career for any length of time, you probably learned about me through Kickstarter. Not only did Monica Leonelle and I write the definitive guide on Kickstarter, but I've personally raised over $500,000 on the platform, been involved in projects that have raised another $400,000, and helped authors raise over $1.2 million for their projects.

I have consulted for Kickstarter, who have sent me to conventions on their behalf, and written articles for their blog. I'm kind of all-in on Kickstarter, is what I'm trying to say. In fact, Kickstarter was indirectly responsible for the Author Ecosystem even existing.

It was looking at specific groups of authors who overperformed and underperformed that got us to start talking about this archetyping system. Well, that and almost blowing up our company because Monica and I were such different ecosystems.

Outside of Substack, I think Kickstarter is the best opportunity for authors to find a new audience and monetize their existing audience. In fact, for most people, Kickstarter will be much more effective, especially at injecting cash into your author business quickly.

So, what is Kickstarter? It's a crowdfunding platform creators use to raise money for creative projects. What makes is different from most other platforms is that you *must* have a creative project in order to launch on their platform.

For most people reading this article, that means a book, but it doesn't have to be a book. You can launch a board game, a play, a music album, drones, pins, or just about anything.

The thing I love about Kickstarter is that it relies on buying triggers in order to maximize attention. For somebody with an "always on" membership like Substack, Kickstarter can activate buyers to make a decision right now.

Specifically, Kickstarter activates the physiological trigger of scarcity.

The truth is that 10 percent of people will like you, 10 percent of people will hate you, and 80 percent will feel nothing for you. Your job is to focus on selling to the 10 percent who like you, while nudging some of that 80 percent from indifference toward liking you.

All of these buying triggers are essential for the long-term growth of your business. They are powerful on their own, but if you can mix them together, you will increase your sales exponentially.

Additionally, Kickstarter has optimized the sales page and checkout experience, which means you don't have to worry about it. Their job is to analyze every campaign to make sure their creators and customers are having a great experience.

While you can create a sales page on your own site, Kickstarter also has a recommendation engine that shows your campaign to customers before and after checkout to help your campaign be found by more people.

I have several sales pages for my own books, but unless I am driving traffic to it myself, there isn't a ton of organic reach happening there. However, with Kickstarter, I consistently get more backers for my projects without advertising.

If you want to learn more about Kickstarter, I highly recommend you read our book or check out the Kickstart Your Book Sales podcast that I co-hosted with Monica. For now, let's dive into how to maximize Kickstarter for each ecosystem.

DESERT

Advantages: Of all the ecosystems, Deserts seem to have the most trouble with Kickstarter. Their entire businesses rely on spotting trends and then taking advantage of them quickly. Kickstarter isn't a platform where you can get arbitrage easily.

In terms of book sales, Deserts are looking for niches where there is considerably more demand than supply. If they can get into a trend early, then they can extract maximum value. Then, when the supply starts to outstrip demand, they move on to the next opportunity.

This is how so many Deserts can thrive without an email list or personal fandom of any kind. They are trying to take advantage of those gaps in the market before they become widespread.

This is antithetical to the Kickstarter ethos, which is what we call a fan-based platform. Kickstarter is great at activating fans, but the algorithm is pretty simple, and the market doesn't change much from month to month.

In fact, a large portion of the indie fiction community has started to ask the question "Is Kickstarter oversaturated?" Since 2023 the average number of campaigns live in the fiction portion of Kickstarter has risen from 6-10 to 100-120.

This would not be a problem for a Forest, who now has tons more authors to share their campaigns with and expand their audience, but for a Desert this saturation of the market is a real concern.

That said, all is not lost. There are a couple of ways that Deserts can use Kickstarter effectively.

The first is when they see a gap in the market and need more money than they have access to at the moment. We know an author who saw a gap in the market at the beginning of the tarot card book and needed $10,000 in order to take advantage of it.

They spun up a campaign and were able to create a thriving business from it. They will probably never use Kickstarter again…unless they see a gap in the market again and need another quick influx of cash.

The second is to spin up a "Forest pen name". Almost all Deserts we meet have a secret Forest pen name they have trouble monetizing because it's a completely different way of thinking. Their Forest stories are off-market and that is the kind of stuff that kills on Kickstarter.

The third is as another distribution channel. My friend runs a very successful publishing company, and launches many of their titles on Kickstarter because "there are buyers there and I like money". Do any of his campaigns crush it? No, but he can bring in an additional $4,000-$10,000 every month to his business, and that's not nothing either. They have a formula they use and don't put a ton of effort into their launches. It just works for them as a distribution channel.

Challenges: The "pump and dump" strategy Deserts use to flood the market at launch with ad dollars and then let the algorithm carry them doesn't work on Kickstarter (or wide retailers, but that's another story). Kickstarter is all about consistent marketing, and unfortunately, there aren't a lot of newsletters or other marketing opportunities for a Kickstarter that are hands-off. So, you're probably going to have to get your hands dirty, at least a bit.

Deserts have problems with Kickstarter because it feels like they have to stop their business cold in order to run one, and that is suboptimal. So, if you want to run a Kickstarter, the most important thing is to find ways to make it a part of your ecosystem without draining you.

GRASSLAND

Advantages: The hardest thing a Grassland ever has to say is "Did you know you can buy this from me?" They are perfectly happy making new content forever and building up incredible goodwill in the community by moving the conversation forward. They are also often thought leaders in their niche or one of the more popular authors in a genre. However, they rely on people just finding their work, instead of being "pushy" or doing a "hard sell".

Here's the thing about making money, though. In order to make sales, sometimes you have to ask for money. Kickstarter is the perfect way to "stand up a tree" as we call it and plant a flag in the ground around your topic.

Grasslands have often talked about their topic or genre for years, and often have hundreds of blog posts or several books. Kickstarter is a way to say, "Hey, look at me. I have this very cool thing I've been working on that I think you'll love".

Kickstarter becomes a great way to cement your leadership on a topic or genre because suddenly for a finite amount of time, all attention turns to you. If you have trouble asking for a sale, using a time-based strategy like Kickstarter is a great way to focus your efforts for a short burst.

While Tundras give 100% effort in short bursts, Grasslands tend to work at 20-50% all the time, releasing things consistently instead of in a frantic burst. For Kickstarter, I recommend harnessing your inner Tundra to push hard on one project for a little while.

It's a bit like popping a balloon. If you lay a balloon on a bed of needles, it won't pop because the force is disbursed. However, if you put the same force into one single needle, the balloon will pop easily.

That said, you can use your natural tendencies to your advantage with Kickstarter, too. For instance, while I prefer 17-20 day campaigns, Monica prefers 45-60 day campaigns where she can take things a bit easier on herself. She will not push her campaigns for several days, or even a week, and then create a flurry of activity.

If you're not one who wants to go all in for a short time, you can schedule a campaign for up to 60 days and just let it build over time with your natural rhythms.

Challenges: The biggest challenge for a Grassland is asking for the sale. Grasslands like to work under the radar, not coming up for air and announcing themselves until they "own the topic". They are a bit like Deserts in that respect. They are looking for the arbitrage of a genre or topic, but instead of hopping off the trend when it gets popular, they surface with 30 books and suddenly they are the dominant force driving the conversation.

I don't recommend Grasslands do more than 1-2 campaigns in a year, and only if it reinforces their topic or genre. Grasslands suffer from "shiny object syndrome" and want to follow every rabbit hole, but Kickstarter is best utilized to draw attention to their thought leadership and reinforce their position in the industry.

We often say that Grasslands are a flywheel without a sales funnel, and Kickstarter gives you a sales funnel.

You need both in your business, and Kickstarter will help you sustain a sales funnel for the long term.

TUNDRA

Advantages: Kickstarter was tailor-made for Tundras, who are basically just living, breathing sales funnels.

If you are a Tundra and you aren't using Kickstarter, you should get on it right now. The first time that I saw Kickstarter, it immediately made sense to me. Generally, Tundras like to exert maximum energy for a short amount of time, which works perfectly with the time-based Kickstarter campaign model.

For Tundras, I recommend working Kickstarter like a fashion designer, in seasons. Pick four times a year you want to "peak" at a launch, spend 17-20 days launching, and then spend the rest of the time recovering and rebuilding your audience for the next launch.

Make sure to vary your launch lengths, too. I find I have about 90 days of launching in me a year, so I make sure to do some shorter campaigns and longer campaigns depending on the amount of money I need to complete a project. I prefer 17-20 day campaigns for most things, but if I have a marketing-heavy launch, or I'm doing a lot of swaps, then I make them 30+ days. The longer the launch, the more chances you have to build a critical mass, but the more it will take out of you.

It's critically important you take time to rest and recover between launches, but if you build it right there is no reason you shouldn't be able to do 4 launches a year with relative ease.

Additionally, you should consider varying your launches. Instead of only launching books, for instance, try launching pins, comics, or other formats to keep engaging new segments of your audience.

Challenges: Tundras love to launch, and they hate to build just as much. The biggest problem Tundras face is that they don't take the time to rest and recover between launches. Tundras burn through more subscribers than any other ecosystem because they are basically one big sales funnel. That means between launches they need to be focused on building their community and finding potential customers more than any other ecosystem.

If you are not building between launches, you will end up launching to a dwindling audience. Then, as you extend out to more launches, you won't be gaining more revenue. Instead, you'll just be fracturing your audience more and more, but making the same money at the end of the day.

If you continue to build between launches, then you'll always have a new audience for your next launch.

Additionally, Tundras need to spend the most time hibernating between launches. You can't give 100% forever. If you do, you'll burn out.

While Grasslands (and Forests) are flywheels without a funnel, Tundras are sales funnels without a flywheel. Augment your launches with either a Grassland or Forest model for your flywheel. Otherwise, you will have trouble retaining a fanbase for the long haul.

FOREST

Advantages: We call Kickstarter a fan-based platform, perfect for activating fans and turning them into buyers, and Forests are great at showering love on their fans. So, Kickstarter is a match made in Heaven for them…or it should be.

However, Forests often position their campaigns like they are talking to somebody who knows all their inside jokes and has read every word they have written, which ends up being very intimidating to new and casual fans.

Forests would have better success if they considered each campaign a chance to onboard new and casual fans into their world. Whenever I check out a campaign from a Forest, my first question is always "Who is this for?"

Almost always it's directed at superfans. That's fine…if you only want superfan backers. However, even superfans probably don't know every inside joke in your universe.

The best use of a Forest's ability to connect with readers is to rely on your fans to guide you to the best kind of campaign to make, and then find a way to create an experience that both superfans and casual readers will love.

You probably have casual readers in your audience who want to go deeper with you, but your huge interconnected universe is imposing. Offering them a beautiful special anniversary edition of your book, with the option to get a cheaper option so they can try it out first, would probably satisfy both hardcore and casual fans.

Either way, make sure to use Kickstarter as a way to celebrate your audience and your fandom. Create a special experience, maybe even an event where they can pick up your books in person, so you can turn those casual readers into superfans and show how welcoming you can be with your work, and how cool it is to be one of your superfans.

Challenges: The biggest challenge to a Forest on any platform is to create low barrier of entry paths for new fans to join the fan club. Kickstarters can be a wonderful way to shower love on your superfans, but you should also use it as a way to onboard people who aren't one of your superfans yet.

The other biggest issue with Forests is going overboard and falling into the red on a campaign because you want to give everything to your readers. Remember to use caution when launching new perks, and understand that revenue is not profit. It's great to give a ton to your fans, but don't fall into debt doing it.

AQUATIC

Advantages: Aquatics have the highest superfan ratio of any ecosystem (even Forests), and they intuitively know how to expand to additional formats, something Tundras should learn to thrive. The one disadvantage to an Aquatic is that they need a lot of money to expand into so many formats, which makes Kickstarter the perfect vehicle to inject capital into your business from your superfans.

Aquatics almost always have one central universe and are trying to expand from there, so I would recommend using Kickstarter as a way to build out your offerings into additional formats from the same world. Aquatics see opportunity everywhere, so the most important thing for an Aquatic to learn is discipline.

Yes, you might want to direct that movie tomorrow, but since it will take $20 million dollars, maybe you should work your way up to that one by offering RPGs, choose-your-own-adventure novels, short films, pins, or other experiences that are easier to expand into than a big movie.

Also, remember that every new format requires you to build an audience from scratch again. Yes, some people will carry over (and those are your superfans), but don't expect the majority of your audience to follow you into a new format. Your goal is to build a robust fanbase full of people who love your universe above everything else, and that will require almost continuous expansion.

Like Tundras, plan to launch in many different formats, except that you will likely only be using Kickstarter when it's time to expand into a new format again. While for a Tundra, Kickstarter is often the end goal, for an Aquatic it should be used strategically, like a Desert, when you see an expansion opportunity.

That doesn't mean you can't go back to the well when you have another product in the same format, but you'll get the most facility by using Kickstarter to onboard people into a new format.

Just remember, every new format is a chance for new fans to jump on board your universe, so don't make it too imposing for people to join. Don't only speak to superfans.

Make sure that you are creating a low barrier of entry for people to fall in love.

Challenges: The biggest challenge for an Aquatic is focus. You need to be singularly focused on one new format at a time, while at the same time allowing for the other formats to grow. You'll probably need to hire some people to keep the old formats growing as you move into others, which is why the Aquatic generally has more partnerships than any other format.

You need to keep all the plates spinning at the same time, and it's very hard to do so and exert enough pressure on any one point to break through in a new format. Once you've done that, try to find other people to spin those plates while you go do the next thing.

FINAL THOUGHTS

Kickstarter can be great regardless of your ecosystem, but if you go into it with the right expectations for your ecosystem, it can supercharge your career and take it to the next level.

If you're looking for a low-barrier of entry way to start with Kickstarter, then there are three campaigns we recommend:

- **Anniversary book** - Pick an anniversary of one of your most successful books and create a special edition hardcover for it. You can offer the works (like sprayed edges) or keep it simple, but all you need is a new cover, new formatting, and (probably) a new proof since we can never have too many of those.

- **"Second Chance" book** - This is a book that was much loved but not much loved by enough people. Often, this is a book launched early in your career that people loved but didn't get the attention it deserved. Now, you are giving it a second chance to succeed. Just like the anniversary book, all you need is a new cover, new formatting, and new proof to get started.

- **Merch** - If you already have an audience, then it's time to think about expanding into other formats. There's probably something fans have asked about for years, and it's a great idea to use Kickstarter as a way to test the waters. Do enough people love the idea enough to pay for it? Set a goal, and tell them if you don't fund, you won't do it. You might fail, but at least then you'll know it's not worth pursuing.

CHAPTER 17

SUBSCRIPTIONS FOR EACH AUTHOR ECOSYSTEM

Building subscriptions into your business is one of the most important ways you can create stability as a writer. Kickstarter launches are great to infuse quick cash into your business, but in order to make long-term plans, it's important to know how much money you have coming into your business predictably every month.

Even though I am very, very, very good at predicting the arc of a Kickstarter campaign, my estimates fall within a range of a few thousand dollars. When you get subscriptions working inside your business, you can start knowing exactly how much money is flowing through your business. More than anything else, this is the best way to combat the feelings of uncertainty that plague almost all writers.

In publishing, I see two types of subscription programs working well right now; publication and association.

In the publication model, customers pay to access the complete archive of a publisher's content. This includes any previously released work and any paid content created specifically for paid members.

You can find the publication model all over the internet, specifically in newspapers. Readers of *The Washington*

Post or *The New York Times* are paying to access the reporting and additional content the newspaper provides.

That does not mean publications only provide articles for their readers. There are plenty of games on *The New York Times* site, and it's very possible to run this kind of model without publishing one word of text.

Take a website like World Anvil. With it, you can create detailed world maps for your universes. You pay a monthly fee, and in return, you receive access to the tool and the ability to use it. You might pay more for a commercial license, but your loyalty isn't really to the brand, it's to the product.

You are likely familiar with the most popular outlet for the publication model among writers. Substack is the perfect venue for a publication model because the publication model relies on SEO and organic reach.

For those of you who don't resonate with this model, the second type of subscription that works well for authors is the association model, where you mainly pay to be part of a group of like-minded humans.

While you would be unlikely to identify yourself as a reader of The Washington Post, you are likely to identify yourself as a member of an association. This model is all about belonging.

When thinking about this model, you can connect it to organizations like Elks Lodge, the Boy/Girl Scouts, or even a bowling league. Yes, we join a bowling league because we like bowling, but we're mostly joining it for access to other like-minded people who have similar interests. If you think of the clubs you joined in high school, it is likely you got as much out of the friendships you made along the way then from the activities you did together.

Unlike publications that get by on virality, associations are all about offering perks to their members to help them connect together and form a deeper connection to the association. For this reason, people using an association model should paywall all or most of their content. Patreon and Ream are perfect places to build an association model because they offer multiple tiers to monetize your more ardent, but less numerous, subscribers.

In general, Deserts and Grasslands tend to resonate with the publication business model while Aquatics and Forests tend to resonate with the associate business model. Tundras can go either way, but they will go that way kicking and screaming because continuity doesn't tend to go well with their launch model.

DESERT

Advantages: The secret power of a Desert is optimization. Deserts can look at a newsfeed and understand the underlying code powering it. If you've ever seen people talk about "gaming the system" that's probably a Desert. They love finding ways to "win the conversation".

Because of this, a publication subscription, especially one built on timeliness, would likely work best for them. While most other ecosystems would burn out releasing a daily newsletter akin to 1440 or Morning Brew, quick turnaround and mining attention while it's hot are two huge skills of a

Desert. Additionally, platforms
like Sparkloop and Beehiiv leverage that virality factor to
help amplify that message through advertising.

The idea of these networks is that publications can offer to
pay a certain amount for every verified subscriber you send
to them. For instance, Bookbub has offered as much as $6 a
subscriber since I've been watching the network closely.

Similarly, you can pay for subscribers other people bring to
your publication as well. The idea is that if you are paying
$2 a subscriber while making $2 a subscriber, you can
basically grow for free. The more often you release
newsletters, the more you can offer to pay because you are
making more from the network with every send.

Most of the biggest newsletters in the world use this
strategy to grow fast, funneling their ad revenue back into
their business to add thousands, even tens of thousands of
new subscribers into their ecosystem every month.

This isn't only for non-fiction authors, either. Today in
Books is a great example of a publication that traffics on
the hot stories of the day but with a bent toward readers.

Challenges: Subscription growth can be slow and churn is
a real challenge, especially for a Desert. Unlike the other
ecosystems, people aren't connecting as much with the
writer as the content, and if somebody serves your
subscribers better, they are prone to leaving quicker for
greener pastures.

For this reason, I would consider making your
subscriptions ad-focused and sponsorship-based instead of
reliant on membership income. I subscribe to dozens of

news organizations to make sure I'm getting full coverage, but I only pay for one.

The strength of a Desert is being able to plug into the "winning" conversation and ride those gains to success fast. Then, they find a new trend and ride that, building momentum by finding that wave consistently.

The association model would likely be the least appealing to a Desert as it requires significantly more love and attention than the publication model. Forests and Aquatics love doting on their subscribers, so they can usually make more per subscriber than a Desert, who will make up in volume what they can't in depth of devotion.

GRASSLAND

Advantages: The publication model is tailor-made for Grasslands, who are built for depth. This model rewards subject expertise and extensive knowledge of a topic, which is exactly how Grasslands "win" the marketing game. Readers are more than happy to geek out on a topic with you all day every day for years.

Additionally, the publication model rewards "putting pennies in the bank" by slowly building their platform over time. Grasslands love content marketing and want their work to be disseminated widely, which is why their work is often antithetical to the association model.

In the association model, most of the benefits are locked behind a paywall, unable to access with the SEO game and bring new people into a Grasslands orbit. Additionally, while a Grassland is happy to speak on a topic, they are more comfortable speaking from a stage or broadcasting their missives than engaging in 1-on-1 conversations with subscribers.

While the Desert and Grassland both prefer the publication model, it's important to note that while a Desert is more like a reporter, finding the best topics of the day and trafficking in virality, a Grassland should think of themselves more like a columnist.

They will do better with longer, more in-depth explainers than quick snippets of the news.

Challenges: Many Grasslands get sucked into the association model, or covet the way a Desert can traffic in immediate virality, but a Grassland has success choosing a topic that will grow in importance over time, and then continuing to provide information about it for years and years as it slowly builds in importance.

Because of that, Grasslands are most inclined to hockey stick growth once the industry gets excited about their topic. However, until then there is likely going to be a lot of slow growth years where you're seeding content all over the internet.

Don't fall into the trap of paywalling your best content. You win by being found by the most people and building your content over time. That's not to say you shouldn't paywall some of your content. However, you should consider having most of your work freely available so that you can create a moat around yourself and any other expert by the depth in which you know your topic.

When we started working together, Monica changed her business to focus more on a live launch model and it didn't work for her. People constantly asked why they couldn't find certain articles or buy certain products. Grasslands are evergreen launchers, and they need to make sure their products are available when somebody finds them.

TUNDRA

Advantages: Tundras can harness excitement and stack tropes on top of each other like no other ecosystem, and that works really well on Kickstarter. However, they prefer to hibernate between launches, which is not ideal for subscriptions

As such, I recommend building a subscription around "PBS-style" pledge drives at certain times of the year to focus your energy. If you think about PBS, you can subscribe at any time, but you only get a tote if you pledge during certain times of the year.

This will allow you to harness excitement in a way that feels good to you, and focus your content creation on those peaks in your schedule. However, instead of launching a product during those peaks, you'll be "launching" your subscription.

This seems to fit in nicely with a Tundra's natural launch, recover, build launch cycle. It would also likely benefit you to get a month ahead of your content so you can turtle when you need to run away from the world.

Challenges: Subscriptions never end…like ever. Tundras are used to building excitement for something and then moving on to the next thing, but with a subscription, they have to keep going constantly. There is always another article due to satisfy the readers, and it's a big shock to the system.

As such, I've had to learn to conserve my energy more because a subscription is a marathon, not a sprint. I've had to find more sustainable ways of doing less, while maintaining the same cadence of my ideal launch cycle.

Additionally, Tundras must remember to reference their vault of information as they continue through their subscription journey. We live to launch and move on, but subscriptions are about referencing and re-referencing your work forever. I found that using sections to help build a big vault of content helps keep continued momentum without needing to constantly be building that excitement every day of my life.

Mostly, you really do have to harness your inner Grassland and become much better at "putting pennies in the bank" in order to maximize your success with subscriptions.

FOREST

Advantages: The association model of subscriptions is all about community, and Forests thrive in those settings. Since the association model is essentially a membership community, Forests should feel right at home on a platform like Patreon or Ream.

Because Forests love engagement, they should focus on platforms that have multiple price points (sorry, Substack) because they will not get a ton of value out of virality. It's not that Forests don't want to grow, but they have a unique bent on the world, which subscribers appreciate, but it won't be everyone's cup of tea.

That said, when somebody finds you and resonates with your work, they'll want to go deep, which means they'll often be willing to make a deeper financial commitment than with a Desert or Grassland. While those two ecosystems traffic in organic reach, a Forest trafficks in resonance and creates a shared language everyone "in the know" can use to talk with each other.

Neither is bad, but you won't win the organic reach game, so why play it?

Instead, play your own game and invite others to play with you as well. While Grasslands don't get much benefit from putting their best work behind a paywall, a Forest likely will because they want to encourage people to go deep with them and give subscribers a safe space to explore their own weirdness.

If you're using Patreon, you might consider connecting it to Wattpad or Royal Road and putting out a serialized project that can help funnel people into your subscription while utilizing the organic reach of those platforms. If you're using Ream, then you can still connect with PayPal through those platforms.

Challenges: Forests have a hard time building momentum anywhere because their interests are wide-ranging and disparate, but if you can do the branding work early and somehow find a way to connect everything together, even in a tenuous way, you'll have more success.

Communities are all about in-jokes and mutually agreed-on norms, but it's important to remember while those things are incredible when you're "in on the joke", they can be intimidating to outsiders. Forests have problems when they fail to look outside their group and be inviting to others, so make sure to be as welcoming to those outside of your community as those inside of it.

If you want to bring in more subscribers, just make sure to give people permission to join and lower the barrier for them to do so. I call this "creating a path". Forests are imposing, but having a well-trodden path makes it inviting for new people to join.

Like a Tundra, you might get a lot of benefit from doing a PBS-style pledge drive, but for a different reason. While a Tundra is doing so in order to traffic in excitement, you are doing it to create a low-barrier-of-entry way to welcome new people into your community and show them how to become a superfan by onboarding them in a low-key way.

AQUATIC

Advantages: Aquatics make inroads all over the internet in a bunch of different formats, but they need a home base that keeps growing over time more than any other ecosystems. While most other ecosystems are focused on 1-2 different formats, an Aquatic wants to do all the things, which means when somebody does resonate with your work, you need to collect them.

Aquatics are masters of delighting their fans, but that delight probably won't carry over to random people who don't know what you're talking about. As such, Aquatics should keep their most delightful work behind a paywall that can be accessed by people who really want to hear what they have to say, maybe offering trials of that work so people can see what is available to them if they become paying members.

Aquatics have the highest ratio of superfans of any ecosystem because once somebody comes into their ecosystem, they are constantly entertained and excited by what they find. Aquatics are constantly doing new and interesting things for their fans that confuse everyone else, which is fine. However, just make sure you keep it contained to the people who will appreciate it.

Challenges: While Aquatics have the highest superfan ratio of any ecosystem, they also tend to have the smallest total audiences. It's the hardest for an Aquatic to find their people because they are trying to create something brand new. Even a Forest is trend-twisting, which involves taking a popular genre and twisting a trope, while an Aquatic is trend-making.

They are likely creating new categories, which makes their jobs even harder. If tech has taught us nothing else, they showed that it's hard to find the innovators and early adopters who can validate your work while you expand it to the majority and eventually the laggards who will build it into a force to be reckoned with in the future. Every subscriber is precious, but you already know that.

You'll probably need Kickstarter, conventions, and other bits of the direct sales landscape to make your ambition goals work, but it's always good to have a place to collect your biggest fans and give them the ability to support your work.

FINAL THOUGHTS

Subscriptions are an amazing and necessary part of every business, but it's not something that you'll start tomorrow and have hundreds of paid members next week.

I see the long-term value in subscriptions, so I'm happy to build for the future, but it is very much a "be kind to future Russell" scenario. I've tried dozens of membership communities, including building my own app, and Substack is the only time I've actually gotten any form of traction.

That doesn't mean Substack will work for you. It might take you ten platforms to find the one that works, or maybe you'll find it tomorrow.

Subscriptions are the definition of go slow to go fast. They don't work until they do, but when they do, they really do. Like anything else, you see growth where you put effort. Even if you don't have a ton of effort to give, the more you can intertwine your subscription into the rest of your business, the better. Subscriptions should be working under everything you do, feeding and slowly growing until it becomes something formidable by itself.

CHAPTER 18

CONVENTIONS, CONFERENCES, AND BOOK SIGNINGS FOR EVERY AUTHOR ECOSYSTEM

Authors who know me probably learned of me through Kickstarter, but Kickstarter was a relatively small part of my business until 2017, and even then it wasn't until 2020 when I started doubling down on Kickstarter. Before then, the vast majority of my fiction income came from conventions.

Live events are festering cesspools of wasted money for most creators. Most creatives know live shows are important for their career, but don't know how to use them to make money or to grow their brand. It ends up being a financial burden instead of a lucrative, money-making opportunity.

The good news is that it's very possible to make money and grow your brand at live shows. If you can do it right, live shows are the absolute best opportunity to quickly build and maintain a passionate audience that will buy from you.

That's the beauty of live events, but it takes incorporating much of what we've talked about previously into the live event experience. It means thinking about live events differently than you do now, and understanding how to make the live event experience work for you.

Live events are the easiest way to build an audience, as well. People are a lot nicer and more engaging in person than they are online. Since you are directly in front of customers with your wares, you can quickly turn somebody from a cold prospect into a warm lead, and even convince them to buy in a single interaction.

The best thing about live events is that everybody who passes your table is a potential customer. They have all paid to get in and decided to walk through your area. In doing so, they have self-selected themselves as being interested in what you have to offer. Now, the trick is just convincing them you are the right vendor for their needs.

Before you read through this section, I highly recommend going back to take notes on the sales funnel, pitching, and mailing list lessons we discussed earlier. I'm not going over them again in this section, and they are critical to your success at live shows.

The most important aspect of live show success is to get in the right mindset before you walk into the door. It's critical that you are prepared to deal with people for ten hours a day for the entire length of the show. Live events will drain you. You need to have a full battery before you walk into the convention center, and you will need time to recharge that battery before the following day.

Everybody has different tricks when it comes to getting in the right mindset. It could mean psyching yourself up in a car for thirty minutes, finding an anchor point with people you know, or picturing everybody naked. Whatever your secret, you need to find the right headspace in order to be successful. All the tactics in the world won't work unless you are mentally ready to employ them.

I know you will want to curl up in a ball and hide after your first unsuccessful pitch, but you have to keep going. Just remember, home is just a few hours away—however, you paid a lot of money to be at the show, and you need to make the most out of it. It's way better to head home with a big wad of cash in your pocket than to have nothing but a hoarse voice to show for your effort.

Of all the elements of direct sales I teach, event sales is easily the one that the least people are interested in, which is wild considering they kept my business going through some very dark times.

I think conventions are an important element of direct sales, and it's important to know how to sell at them in ways that best fit your ecosystem. So, I'm going to lay out the best strategies I have found that would work for each type.

For the sake of this article, I'm going to define conferences, conventions, and book signings as three distinct pieces.

- **Conferences** - These are events set up to learn about an industry, with very little selling going on. There are likely vendors at these events, but they are mainly there to answer questions and set meetings for future sales. Conferences include events like ALA, Bookexpo, 20books, NINC, and the Future of Publishing Mastermind, but also exist in every industry. Events like WorldCon and World Fantasy Convention are a hybrid of the two, but I believe they call on the conference side.

- **Conventions** - These are events where you set up to sell books. These include events like SDCC, NYCC, Phoenix Fan Fusion, Readers Take Denver, and DragonCon, but I'm also going to throw swap meets, flea markets, street festivals, and the like into these because the vibe is more sales-forward.
- **Book Signings** - These are events where you go to a bookstore or library and sign your books, either alone or with a small group of other authors. I'm not going to single these out below much because they can be beneficial to all ecosystems.

Finally, people often ask which events I recommend and I can't tell you that since my experience was defined by my ecosystem. Your experience will be vastly different than mine.

DESERT

Advantages: Deserts are the ecosystem with the least interest in meeting fans and building an audience, so it might at first seem like a poor fit to add events into your catalog, but there are a couple of things that could make event sales work for you.

First, since Deserts generally aim their books at the center of the Bell Curve to appeal to the most people, Deserts have the best ability to hire help to run their booths for them. They might not even show up, since their books are designed to sell themselves. Other ecosystems have a hard time hiring staff to work for them because their books sell at least partially because they are the ones who wrote them.

Not true for Deserts. For Deserts, the appeal of their books is that they are the perfect encapsulation of a genre or trope, so they should be able to sell without the author even being present. This is one of the reasons that Deserts make great publishers because they create experiences that exist beyond any single author.

Additionally, while most other ecosystems should focus on very niche shows where they can find their people, Deserts can usually expand out well beyond that into the flea market, swap meet, and street festival circuit more easily. In general, these events are filled with middle of the Bell Curve readers who want easy-to-consume books that make them feel a certain way inside.

Finally, if you choose to go into the convention circuit, then a Desert can take in the most popular items at an event and learn how to attract the most people to their table with additional merch or special edition covers that speak to the audience without them having to say a word.

As for conferences, Deserts are best at attending to collect data, watch, and learn. They won't get a lot of value speaking at conferences because revealing their secrets would diminish the arbitrage they traffic in for their success. However, people tend to reveal their best secrets in person, and this is like gold for Deserts.

Challenges: Deserts are generally opposed to building audiences, speaking to people, or "dancing for dollars". So, they often come across as surly instead of inviting. All they want to do is write their books in peace, so if you do decide to attend conferences or conventions, especially as a vendor, just remember that you are part of the experience, and you need to put on a good show if you want to make sales.

Events are a microcosm of the overall audience. If you start to cater to them, you'll miss out on the trends of the overall market and it can seriously affect your sales. I've made lots of mistakes by tailoring books to event buyers at the expense of my online sales. That said, you should at least have special edition covers for your books at conventions because those buyers prefer uniqueness over the homogeneity of retailer platforms.

GRASSLAND

Advantages: Since a Grassland's superpower is depth and owning a topic, they will get the biggest advantage of being seen at events catering to their topic. In fact, they should try to speak everywhere they possibly can, as they are trafficking in authority. Every time a new event that allows you to speak is on some level bestowing their blessing on you as an expert, the more audiences you can get in front of, the more authority you will build.

The secret to this is hyper-focusing on your topic. If you are talking about self-publishing, then going to ALA really won't help you at all, because libraries almost exclusively order from Ingram or similar distributors. Similarly, if you are a mid-tier publisher looking to network with bookstores and libraries, 20books Vegas would be a terrible show for you to attend or speak at, because it's all about self-publishing.

I'm talking about publishing here, but my wife does shows hyper-targeted to BCBAs and ABA, and there are similar industry shows for just about every topic from tractors to plumbing to doctors.

For fiction authors, your strength is in having a massive catalog of books in one world, so it will benefit you most to go to places that are hyper-specific to audiences that want your books, even if they are smaller than other ecosystems would benefit from with their books. This is because if you can make one sale, you'll probably sell your whole catalog of books. I highly recommend looking into Dropcards and offering all your books digitally. That way you don't have to carry a thousand books across your epic series.

While I normally recommend that a fiction author not do anything less than a 10,000-person convention, if you can find one laser-focused on your genre, then you'll probably become the most popular author at that event, especially if you speak on a panel. Even as a fiction author, it's critical that you speak on panels about your topic depending on the genre because you also traffic in authority.

Challenges: It's much more exhausting to speak at a show than anyone realizes. I spend the same amount of energy walking 10,000 steps and speaking for one hour. While it's really exciting to be asked to speak at a conference, make sure to be judicious with your energy. Additionally, it's easy to get charmed by shows and let it blind you to online audience building or any of the other ways you should be building your list.

It's really easy at conferences to blend into the crowd, and Grasslands risk being swept up by the crowd if they don't speak up. Large events might not be advisable if you aren't willing to take advantage of the large numbers by inviting them into your universes.

I know a lot of Grasslands who make their living traveling the conference or convention circuit and neglect building their own audience, which makes them dependent on the conference. If it ever stops existing or gets worse, then their business dries up.

TUNDRA

Advantages: If Tundras traffic in excitement, conventions are excitement on steroids. Because Tundras like to exert maximum energy for short bursts, conferences are the perfect outlet for that energy. As long as they remember to rest between events to recover, they can basically just keep running conferences at regular intervals between Kickstarter or other launches.

Since Tundras are often the loudest, most exciting thing around, it's easy for a Tundra to stand out from the crowd and make money at a show even if everyone else is floundering. Their ability to trope stack also allows them to tailor their pitches to different customers, highlighting different aspects of their book depending on what each reader likes.

Additionally, Tundras are the ultimate BOFU (Bottom of the FUnnel) superstars, so they can create packaged offers designed to sell. All of this means that Tundras more than any other ecosystem should look for events with lots of traffic, so they can have the most conversations with the most readers. This doesn't mean going anywhere where there are a lot of readers. I've made that mistake before, but if there's the option of several similar events, default to the biggest one where you can get the most traction.

For conferences, you want to make sure you're on as many panels and workshops as possible, so you can capture the excitement of the attendees and get them to take action. Make sure to have some sort of lead magnet or offer so you can get your audience into your own funnel.

Challenges: Tundras are all about big energy investments to secure big wins, so small events are kind of the death of a Tundra. You still have to expend a ton of energy, but you don't get anywhere near the ROI for your time as you get at big events. Other ecosystems can go on energy saver or low-power mode, but not Tundras.

You also have to remember to recover between shows. You should have at least a 2-week break between shows, but hopefully longer. It seems like 10-12 big shows a year is a good clip for a Tundra. Just make sure the juice is worth the squeeze.

FOREST

Advantages: Forests are great at making everyone in their community feel welcome and a conference or convention is a great way to bring everyone together at one time and invite new people to join you. Forests radiate warmth and are great at engagement, so if they can get somebody to stop at their table or engage them in conversation, they will do great at shows.

However, often Forests don't make the first move. They prefer people to identify as their perfect customers before they engage, so they lose a lot of potential fans who are just casually browsing and don't show that immediate enthusiasm. Forests don't care much for casual things, especially fandom. They focus their attention on people who self-identify as already choosing to enter a Forest's orbit.

On top of that, Forest authors are often introverts outside of their communities, so they shy away from engaging until somebody is bought in, which means they can get drowned out at big events. Instead, a Forest should make their table as welcoming as possible and present a low-barrier-of-entry way to get people excited about their work on a small level. Yes, you want to have something for your superfans, but you should also provide ways for new readers to enter your ecosystem easily.

Think about welcoming everyone with a smile and interacting with as many people in conversation as possible. Additionally, you'll likely want to avoid broad shows like SDCC and focus on ones that are smaller and allow for long conversations with your potential readers, unless you can find ways to create a more intimate experience inside of the larger conference or convention atmosphere.

When you're at a conference, make sure you create ways to meet up with your people, either specifically through your own coordinated events or more generally by providing safe spaces for people in your perfect audience to connect together in event-sponsored meet-ups. The power of your community is in that shared language, and the more your people have chances to connect together and expand your message, the more successful you will be at any event.

You might also consider founding your own conference filled with just your readers to give everyone a safe space to gather and express their inner weirdo. If not, you can consider any conference a chance to build a narrative around your fandom and find your people by the end of it. Start broad on the first day and narrow your focus by the end to bring more ardent fans into your universe.

Challenges: Forests are great at welcoming their people, but they tend to be imposing to people who haven't bought into their worlds yet. Forests more than any other ecosystem need to open up and become super welcoming to everyone that passes their table, not only superfans. It's an amazing experience to watch a Forest talk to somebody already excited to be around them, but the excitement dries up if somebody doesn't know their world yet.

That makes sense because if you're used to speaking to excited and enthusiastic readers, coming across one who doesn't know you from a stranger is off-putting and jarring. It's natural to want to retreat to your community for support, but events are great for breaking you out of your comfort zone and attracting new readers. Once you have them, you'll create lifelong fans. Don't be scared to reach out beyond your comfort zone.

AQUATIC

Advantages: Aquatics are masters at delighting their audience. While Tundras sell through excitement, Aquatics sell through delighting their fans with different formats and knowing them so well that they can create superfans almost at will if they get in front of the right customers. Aquatics have the highest percentage of superfans of any ecosystem. However, they also tend to have very small audiences because they are hyper-focused on those people who resonate with their message.

Like Forests, Aquatics should focus on how to delight the most people at a conference if they want to have success. Since they are usually delightful, this means if they extend themselves beyond just their superfans and create ways for readers to join their universe, they will succeed. The great thing about Aquatics is that they already have a ton of formats that are tailored to so many buyers, so they can lean on that to bring people in from a wider pool than just readers.

Like Grasslands, it's probably best for them to focus on events that are very tailored to their specific audience because they'll be able to convert smaller audiences better than any other ecosystem, even if they don't have a ton of content. Since they are trying to create a trend from nothing, most people will pass by their booth at a large, unfocused show. If they are able to have long conversations with a select group of people, they will thrive.

Even more than Forests, Aquatics should think about forming their own conference or convention. Their people will pay top dollar to have an exclusive experience with them, and Aquatics will rise to the challenge to create something unique and wonderful.

Challenges: Aquatics speak the language of their universe, which is isolating to most people they meet at a conference. They need to find ways to expand their message and broaden the appeal if they want to bring in new readers. Aquatics don't really care about new readers, but you can't get superfans if you don't get new readers, and you can't get new readers if you don't expand your message to give them permission to join your world.

More than any other ecosystem, Aquatics risk being drowned out at an event because their topic is usually very niche. The more they can tack that message to an overall topic or theme with more resonance, the more people they will attract and the more success they will have. They already know how to treat their superfans. They just need to find ways to bring new fans into their universe.

FINAL THOUGHTS

As I mentioned at the top, I didn't mention book signings much above. I highly recommend you go into your local bookshops and libraries to schedule events with them. Most of them have events throughout the year you can join for free or cheap and they can become excellent advocates for your work.

There is no doubt that these types of events are time-consuming and energy-draining. You need to take time to recover from them and plan for that time. However, they are also the quickest way to inject much-needed enthusiasm (and revenue) into your business.

While it takes 7-14 touchpoints to make a sale online, you can drastically reduce that at an in-person event, often down to a single conversation. We are social creatures and like to do business with people we meet in person over those we only see online. That is the power of these events.

Additionally, since you are surrounded by other people who are all on a similar journey as you, or at least resonate with the same kind of stuff, there is a shared language that develops, and shared experiences bond people together.

Just remember, events are only one pillar of direct sales. While they can be used often, as I used to do 30-40 events in a year, it's also very effective to pick and choose your events carefully around launch events, or lulls in your years to inject excitement into your business when you need it most.

CHAPTER 19

MAXIMIZING SUBSTACK FOR EACH ECOSYSTEM

Most authors I talk with ask some form of the question, "How did you succeed on Substack?" Of course, what they really mean is, "How can I succeed at Substack?"

While I can't give you personalized advice, because this is a pre-written column and you are a living, breathing human reading this asynchronously, the next best thing is to show you how each ecosystem can best utilize Substack to grow their own author career.

I have spent hundreds of hours on Substack trying to learn everything I could about the platform. Meanwhile, we've talked to hundreds of authors about their ecosystems. Together, I've molded those two conversations to create an overview of how I think each ecosystem can utilize Substack.

One thing I will say is that if you're looking for fiction, there are roughly 300 fiction publications that write fiction. I have a ton of fiction available in my publication, but there is not the same amount of fiction as there is in nonfiction. Luckily, the fiction community here is hugely supportive and they are great about supporting each other.

However, if you are specifically looking for a deep well of fiction readers/authors to mine immediately, you will likely be disappointed. If you're looking for a supportive, growing community, then you're in the right place. Fiction is in its infancy here, but I think it will grow into something magical with time and support.

DESERT

Advantages: The secret power of a Desert is optimization. Deserts can look at a newsfeed and understand the underlying code powering it. If you've ever seen people talk about "gaming the system" that's probably a Desert. They love finding ways to "win the conversation".

When you start looking at Notes, the first thing a Desert will realize is that the algorithm powering Substack is very basic. It's not quite Facebook circa 2004, but it does absolutely remind me of 2010-2012 Facebook, and a lot of the strategies that no longer work on other platforms still work here.

For instance, while the feed is not chronological, every time your post is commented on, you'll be boosted to the top of people's feeds. Additionally, commenting on other people's posts helps you be seen by more people as well because the last comment is shown to people scrolling. If you can make charming and well-thought-out comments, you will start to see your subscriber count going up.

On top of that, attending events and engaging in the conversation can lead to significant growth in your publication, especially if you are in a popular niche like self-help, psychology, food, or author services.

Challenges: Growth on Substack is slow. Deserts often tire of platforms where they can't see exponential growth quickly and Substack is a very small platform compared to TikTok, Amazon, Facebook, Instagram, etc. The strength of a Desert is being able to plug into the "winning" conversation and ride those gains to success fast. Then, they find a new trend and ride that, building momentum by finding that wave consistently.

There is absolutely a prevailing narrative on Substack, but while a bigger platform will have a dozen or more conversations happening at one time between millions of people, Substack usually has 1-2 between thousands, so you'll have to plant more in one of a couple of categories to have fast growth.

Additionally, Substack rewards subject expertise. Deserts are incredible at writing on any subject as long as it's popular. They take joy in the writing work as much as, or more than, the topic. While Substack certainly has "general" Substack publications that deal with a lot of topics, they generally have a theme or tone that unites them. For a Desert who's used to donning a hundred personalities depending on the job, it can feel limiting.

GRASSLAND

Advantages: Substack is tailor-made for Grasslands, who are built for depth. Substack rewards subject expertise and extensive knowledge of a topic, which is exactly how Grasslands "win" the marketing game. Readers are more than happy to geek out on a topic with you all day every day for years.

Additionally, Substack rewards "putting pennies in the bank" by slowly building your platform over time. There are multiple articles about Substack success that started with somebody investing in their publication for years and slowly building over time until they started to see exponential growth almost overnight.

While this might seem like a nightmare scenario for other ecosystems, it's often how Grasslands prefer to exist. They have no problem talking about a trend they spot for years before they reap the rewards when people finally catch up to them.

Additionally, one of the best growth strategies on Substack is to incorporate ongoing conversations into articles while still keeping them on-topic, which is something Grasslands have the preternatural ability to do naturally.

Challenges: Substack is great for depth, but there is also an ongoing conversation happening through Notes and events like Office Hours. The biggest challenge for Grasslands is the inability or unwillingness to join that ongoing conversation. Most Grasslands came to Substack in order to write long and nerd out about their topic, but they miss plugging into the conversation to help improve the timeliness of their writing.

Many Grasslands are so busy going deep on a topic that they miss the ability to influence that ongoing conversation. While the conversation on Notes might not always be about your topic, that's no reason to avoid trying to influence it. I pick up subscribers every day by communicating with them on Notes, Plus, often the posts I make on Notes become the seeds of future articles.

I do work in the author growth space, though, so often by simply existing in this space I can find new subscribers, but that only worked because I embraced my inner Grassland and found a topic with a lot of depth that I thought would be of interest to the Substack audience for a long time.

Don't forget, any social media platform is best utilized by finding the intersectionality between your interests and how the conversation works on the platform already. If you can plug into that conversation by harnessing your inner Desert, then your natural strengths as a Grassland will help you carry the day.

TUNDRA

Advantages: Tundras can harness excitement and stack tropes on top of each other like no other ecosystem, and that works really well on Substack. The conversation on Substack is often cyclical, so if you can harness your inner Grassland and write evergreen articles about those topics, you will be able to bring people into your ecosystem while their excitement is at its highest.

You have to be careful not to sound like a broken record pitching the same thing over and over, but as long as you infuse everything with excitement, you should be able to keep your content fresh.

Tundras love figuring out how to position their work in the market, and it was easy to distinguish myself from other publications by the sheer length and depth of my articles (they tend to be 5,000+ words). I try to stack 2-3 popular evergreen tropes into each article so that as many people can get value from a single piece of content as possible.

My promotion strategy looks a lot like a mini version of the rolling waves I usually talk about which are ideal for a Tundra. Every article releases on Wednesday, and I crescendo my marketing then. I have also found a lot of value in creating a weekly roundup with dozens of other articles I loved to help harness other people's excitement to help drive marketing for my own articles.

Challenges: Subscriptions never end…like ever. Tundras are used to building excitement for something and then moving onto the next thing, but with Substack, they have to keep going constantly. There is always another article due to satisfy the readers, and it's a big shock to the system.

As such, I've had to learn to conserve my energy more because Substack is a marathon, not a sprint. Instead of building up huge excitement for every launch, I've had to find more sustainable ways of doing less, while maintaining the same cadence of my ideal launch cycle.

Additionally, Tundras must remember to reference their vault of information as they continue through their Substack journey. We live to launch and move on, but Substack is about referencing and re-referencing your work forever. I found that using sections to help build a big vault of content helps keep continued momentum without needing to constantly be building that excitement every day of my life.

Mostly, you really do have to harness your inner Grassland and become much better at "putting pennies in the bank" in order to maximize your success with Substack. Likely, you will also get a lot of value from doing PBS-style pledge drives a few things a year to focus attention on Substack to harness than excitement, which would be a launch strategy uniquely suited to Tundras.

FOREST

Advantages: Substack is all about community, and Forests thrive in those settings. Since Substack is essentially a membership community, Forests should feel right at home with things like Recommendations and using sections to increase value to paid members.

Additionally, the Substack community is very interested in reading publications with unique voices, which is where Forests shine. The more unique you can make your articles, the better chance you have for success. This is a huge boon for Forests, who win at marketing by embracing their inner weirdo.

Forests are also very concerned with improving the human experience for others, which fits in very well with the ethos of Notes and events like the discontinued Office Hours. The more "love" you can shower to connect with people on an individual level, the more success you will have, and that's one of a Forest's biggest strengths.

Challenges: Forests have a hard time writing anything that is not 100% aligned with their inner north star. They are the opposite of Deserts in that respect, but part of succeeding on Substack is being part of the ongoing narrative on the platform.

The more you can merge your own north star with what's happening in the overall conversation happening on the platform, the quicker you will have success.

Forests have a hard time building momentum anywhere because their interests are wide-ranging and disparate, but if you can do the branding work early and somehow find a way to connect everything together, even in a tenuous way, you'll have more success.

Communities are all about in-jokes and mutually agreed-on norms, but it's important to remember while those things are incredible when you're "in on the joke", they can be intimidating to outsiders. Forests have problems when they fail to look outside their group and be inviting to others, so make sure to be as welcoming to those outside of your community as those inside of it.

One of the major reasons to be on Substack is for the organic growth you get through their recommendation engine and network effects. Make sure to use them effectively to scale. Otherwise, you might find more success on Patreon, which was designed to shower love on people already in on the joke.

AQUATIC

Advantages: Aquatics want to do all the things all the time, and Substack has lots of formats to play with, including their own podcasting system. They allow you to set up sections to silo off different projects from each other and play with transmedia across audio, video, photography, art, comics, and text.

There are tons of different subcommunities on Substack that you can use to build your publication. You can create a photography project for #photostack, a film for #filmstack, a comic for #comicstack, a choose-your-own-adventure for #gamestack, and just keep creating new ways to bring people into your universe. None of these niches are particularly huge, but together they can add up to a powerful audience.

You can also use the hunger for new content in these smaller audiences to help build excitement for your projects with a lot of organic reach. Then, when they're inside your universe, they will find how many other amazing formats and projects they can sink their teeth into in order to fall deeper in love with your brand.

Challenges: Substack only allows one price point for subscriptions, but Aquatics generally have multiple formats that require different price points, so it will be hard to find one price point to service their whole audience. One thing they can think about is using their Founding member tier for their more resource-intensive formats. Or, they can simply price their whole publication at a higher level ($20+) than would be normal with other ecosystems ($5-$10/mo is the norm).

Additionally, while there are different niches within Substack, Aquatics might not be able to enter into the main conversation often enough to scale fast. With a platform like Reddit or Facebook, even the small niches are huge, but with Substack, there are generally only 1-2 main conversations happening at the same time.

Hopefully, you already have a ton of different formats to play with before entering the Substack ecosystem, because it would take a ton of paid members in order to scale beyond the written word without also utilizing something like Kickstarter or Patreon to fill out your ecosystem. However, if you want to find a place to create one monster audience from a bunch of formats, then Substack could work great for you.

FINAL THOUGHTS

Substack can work for any ecosystem, but it works even better if you can harness a little bit of every ecosystem. If you can mine the conversations to stay on top of the reader's mind like a Desert while also harnessing your inner Grassland to go deep on a niche, you will have a powerful combination for success. If you can additionally stack evergreen topics and harness excitement like a Tundra while building a community like a Forest and expanding out to different formats like an Aquatic, you'll do even better. It's a bit like Voltron. Those kitties are powerful alone, but together they are unstoppable.

There is a ton of good on Substack, but it's not a platform you'll start tomorrow and have hundreds of paid members next week. I brought 25,000 emails in April 2023 and I didn't have 100 paying members until September 2023. Even with 450 paying members, I only made $12,000/year since I offer such steep discounts during my pledge drives. I've been pushing hard on Substack since for a while, and while we've made tens of thousands of dollars on other platforms this year, my gross annual revenue is tracking below $4,000 on Substack.

I see the long-term value in Substack, so I'm happy to build for the future, but it is very much a "be kind to future Russell" scenario. Still, I've tried dozens of membership communities, and this is the only time I've actually gotten any form of traction. Add on the fact that I gain between 500-600 organic subscribers a month through network effects and recommendations alone with no financial investment and it makes a powerful case for me to spend a lot of time here.

However, the more flexible you can be, the more successful you will be here, and the quicker you will attain that success. That said, you can be very successful doubling down on any ecosystem if you give yourself time to build your publication.

CHAPTER 20

WHAT NOW?

If you've read this far, I want to thank you for your persistence and perseverance. I know that learning about business isn't any creator's favorite thing to do in the world; however, just by reading this book, you are so much further ahead than most creatives on this planet.

I would say to give yourself a round of applause, but I've worked very hard throughout this book not to be cheesy and don't want to ruin it now.

Well, maybe just a little applause would be okay. Not too long, though, because now the real work begins.

That's right…work.

As much knowledge as I crammed into this book, it's truly just a primer to gear you up for a lifelong pursuit of learning about the business of art. The goal of this book is to give you the necessary tools so you can go out there and build the foundation of a creative career.

It's not an endpoint. It's a beginning.

You made it to the end of this book. Now, you are prepared for the horrible and yet consistent world of late-stage capitalism. However, you still have to live in it.

This book is based on The Author Ecosystems Archetyping System methodology created and designed by Russell

Nohelty and Monica Leonelle. All rights reserved.

If you loved this book, I hope you go check out *The Author Stack,* my weekly newsletter that goes into even more depth about how to build your creator career.

https://www.theauthorstack.com/

As a paid member, you get access to a ton of my previous work, including fiction, non-fiction, courses, and more.

RESOURCES:

- *How to Build Your Creative Career*
- *How to Become a Successful Author*
- *Advanced Growth Tactics for Authors*
- *Get Your Book Selling on Kickstarter*
- *Get Your Book Selling on Facebook*
- *Get Your Book Selling with Cross-Promotion*
- Get Your Book Selling at Events and Signings
- *Get Your Book Selling in Print*
- Create Profitable Facebook Ads course
- Fund Your Book with Kickstarter course
- How to set up and run an awesome anthology course
- How to run a viral giveaway to build your mailing list
- Write a Great Novel course
- How to Build an Audience from Scratch minicourse
- 10x your productivity course
- Lessons and lectures
- Interview archive
- Complete Creative data archive
- Income reports since 2018
- Script library

There's probably even more now since I update it every couple of months.

You can also find my work at: www.russellnohelty.com

Feel free to email me at russell@wannabepress.com and let me know what you think, and please leave a review. The only way I know I should keep writing these kinds of books is from your reviews and kind words.

Find more of my work at my blog:

www.theauthorstack.com

Find all my work at my website:

www.russellnohelty.com

Bookbub:

https://www.bookbub.com/profile/russell-nohelty